"We'll be getting married within the month and no one needs to know that neither of us is wild about the idea."

"I can't do that!" Leila protested. "I won't. Women don't coerce a man into marriage these days because there's a baby on the way."

"I don't understand your reluctance, my dear," Dante said bitterly. "You claim you still have some feelings for me. You're expecting my children. You need my help. And all I'm demanding by way of collateral on my investment is that you become Mrs. Dante Rossi. What's so difficult about that?"

She's sexy,
successful...
and
PREGNANT!

Relax and enjoy our new series of stories about spirited women and gorgeous men, whose passion results in pregnancies...sometimes unexpected! Of course, the birth of a baby is always a joyful event, and we can guarantee that our characters will become besotted moms and dads—but what happened in those nine months before?

Share the surprises, emotions, dramas and suspense as our parents-to-be come to terms with the prospect of bringing a new little life into the world.... All will discover that the business of making babies brings with it the most special love of all....

Look out next month for:
The Unexpected Father by Kathryn Ross
Harlequin Presents® #2022

CATHERINE SPENCER

Dante's Twins

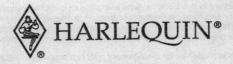

TORONTO • NEW YORK • LONDON
AMSTERDAM • PARIS • SYDNEY • HAMBURG
STOCKHOLM • ATHENS • TOKYO • MILAN • MADRID
PRAGUE • WARSAW • BUDAPEST • AUCKLAND

ISBN 0-373-12016-8

DANTE'S TWINS

First North American Publication 1999.

CHAPTER ONE

THEY made love on the third day, less than seventy-two hours after they met. "Come with me," he said urgently.

Without hesitation she took the hand he held out in invitation. "Yes."

And just that easily, while others in the group dozed through the worst of the afternoon heat or swam desultory lengths up and down the pool, he spirited her away up one of the trails leading to the middle of the island.

She knew what the outcome of their clandestine rendezvous would be. It wasn't a question of right or wrong, of imprudence or immorality; it was a matter of destiny. She'd belonged to him from the moment he'd set eyes on her that first night and the only miracle was that they'd waited this long to consummate their union.

Fingers linked tightly in his, she followed him, stepping nimbly to avoid the lush jungle growth that impeded the way and hid their escape from speculative or hostile observers at the plantation house. Eventually they came to a place beside a spring bubbling out from beneath a slab of rock, where the earth was tufted with moss and sweet-smelling flowers swayed from vines strung overhead like a canopy.

Turning to face her, he spoke her name, "Leila...?" but it was not the voice of a CEO addressing his employee. It was thick and husky with passion, a lover's voice.

"I'm here," she said.

At that, he drew her to him until not the most slender beam of sunlight could come between them, and lowered his lips to hers.

How could she possibly have grown into womanhood and not known that a huge part of her life lay untouched by real passions? Or deluded herself into thinking she knew what being kissed by a man was all about?

His mouth seduced her completely in less time than other men had taken to ask her out to dinner. The person she'd been, the one she thought she knew, exploded in a series of tiny detonations that started where his lips touched hers and rippled throughout her body until not a part of her remained unmoved.

She might have looked the same to the untutored eye but, in that instant, the womanly pattern of her changed forever. Her focus altered, her instincts grew sharper. A more primitive awareness shaped her intelligence. And her heart…oh, it had ceased to be hers to control three days before.

Lifting his head, he broke the kiss just long enough to ask, "Are you sure?"

Did the sun rise in the east? Soft and moist and willing, she swayed in his embrace and surrendered her soul. "Never more sure, Dante. I will follow wherever you lead."

He gathered a fistful of her hair and tugged her closer to let her learn how much he desired her. "I'll never give you cause for regret, my love," he vowed, and renewed the kiss, more deeply this time.

She opened her lips and let her tongue mate with his in an eager, pulsing rhythm that even she, virgin that she was, recognized as bold acceptance of his invitation to share the greatest intimacy a woman could know with a man.

His hands touched her, eager to discover her flesh. She did not remember sinking to the mossy ground or how she came to be naked or when he threw aside his own clothes. Like everything else about her life that had gone before, it did not matter. The ordinary world narrowed, too pale an entity to compete with the paradise he invoked.

His heavy-lidded gaze devoured her, blazing a trail for his tongue to follow down her throat and along her collarbone to her breasts where he lingered, stirring her to aching unfamiliar pleasure. His hand dipped to her abdomen, the fingers splaying wide to seek the angled crease of her thigh where it joined her torso, then probing her most secret part and...oh!

Sensing the sudden quiver of shock that fluttered within her, he paused and lifted his head. "This is your first time, isn't it?" he said on a note of wonder.

At her nod, he blew out a steadying breath and, turning on his side, he curved his hands around her and stroked the length of her spine, quieting her fears. "Don't be afraid, Leila," he said. "I'll never hurt you."

Of course he wouldn't. He was the man she'd been waiting for all her life, the one with whom she'd share eternity. She had nothing to fear.

Wanting to please him as he pleased her, she pressed her lips to his chest and left a warm, damp imprint there to let him know her moment of panic had passed. Beneath her mouth his heart jerked a response, rapid, uneven.

This time when he touched her, her vision narrowed, isolating her in a space just short of heaven and leaving her reaching...trembling...wanting....

Disembodied, her voice called to him, begging for something she couldn't begin to define. "Dante, please...help me..."

At her words, he lowered his head and found her with his tongue, and she forgot to be shocked or modest or restrained. She simply melted like honey.

The tension within her coiled unbearably until, with one last powerful wrench, it burst free of itself, and all she could do was dig her nails into Dante's shoulders and pray that she would not drop off the edge of the earth and lose him forever.

For a moment he crushed her to him, anchoring her to reality. Then, eyes half closed and chest heaving, he rose above her, all proud masculine strength. Firmly, he nudged apart her knees with one of his own.

He has stolen my soul. I cannot give him more, she thought helplessly.

And was wrong. Because she had not begun to give; she had only received and mistakenly believed *that* to be the greatest pleasure a woman could experience. But her body knew differently, expanding to accept him and closing around him, sleek and tight with welcome.

The rhythm began again, frenzied and untamed. It possessed her, seizing the air in her lungs, paralyzing her heart, and summoning a devastation that would have terrified her had he not held her so securely.

She cried out his name again, wept into his shoulder, struggled to soar with him and suddenly felt herself explode into a million fragments. And through it all he rode with her, welding her with his heat until she was whole again and flooding her with his loving.

For long minutes after that, she heard only the burbling of the spring. Felt only the spongy resilience of the moss beneath her and the weight of him above her. Saw behind her closed eyelids only the muted brightness of the sun spearing through the trees.

Finally, he spoke. "You are beautiful," he said, in the same passion-charged voice he'd used before. "Beautiful through and through. And you are mine."

"Yes," she sighed. "I love you, Dante."

It never occurred to her to doubt the truth of her statement, any more than it occurred to her to question the truth of his. He was her soul mate. He would never lie to her, nor she to him.

"I remember when I used to be assigned to this end of the house. Those were the old days, before the company started going to hell in a handcart.''

With night having fallen swiftly, as it did in the trop-
ics, the only light outside came from the kerosene
torches in the courtyard below. But she didn't need to
see the face belonging to the voice to recognize the
speaker as Carl Newbury.

For one startled moment after she stepped out of the
bathroom, she thought he was actually in her suite and
speaking to her. In fact, he was leaning on the veranda
railing next door, his words directed at someone in the
room behind.

Uncomfortable at finding herself unwitting eavesdrop-
per, Leila crossed to the slatted French doors, intending
either to close them or make her presence known, when
he spoke again.

''The last person I expected would be taken in by such
a blatant come-on is Dante Rossi. I thought he had more
smarts than that, but I guess when sex enters the picture...''

''It's gone that far?'' another male voice exclaimed.

''You witnessed the way they went sneaking off after
lunch today,'' Newbury sneered, pausing to slurp noisily
at whatever he was drinking. ''And you saw them come
back, and the furtive way she scurried around to the back
entrance while he strolled along the front terrace, bold
as brass, so you tell me.''

Aghast to realize she and Dante were the subject of
so unsavory an exchange, Leila froze on the threshold
of her own veranda, hidden by the gauzy white curtains
fluttering in the breeze from the ceiling fan.

''They *were* holding hands,'' the unseen other party
replied, and although she couldn't identify him, the fact
that, like her, he'd been assigned to the back wing of
the house suggested he didn't rate Carl Newbury's executive status. ''Still, to assume that means he got her
in the sack within a couple of days of meeting her is a

bit far-fetched, surely? Dante's a good-looking man and women obviously find him attractive, but he doesn't strike me as a playboy.''

''Normally he isn't—at least not when he's dealing with ladies. But let's face it, pal, Leila Connors-Lee is no lady, for all her fancy airs. She got herself hired in the first place by flashing her legs and batting her long eyelashes at Gavin Black. But he's married and old enough to be her father, so she looked around for bigger fish to land and it looks as if she's hooked Dante.''

''But he never mixes business with pleasure. His private life is just that. Private.''

''It used to be.'' Ice clattered against crystal, followed by the gurgle of liquid being poured. ''But I've thought for a while that his judgment's been off, and I guess this proves it.''

''He's got too many brains to be taken in by a pretty face.''

Newbury's laugh made Leila's skin crawl. ''We both know a man's brain isn't what drives him when sex enters the picture, especially not when it's handed to him on a plate.''

''Ah!'' Afraid she might be sick, Leila pressed the palm of her hand to her mouth. She knew she'd alienated Carl Newbury the first week she'd been hired, and she knew it went beyond her having taken over a position he'd earmarked for one of his friends, so she didn't expect him to regard her with particular favor. But that he was prepared to carry the grudge this far left her reeling.

''Well, there's not much we can do about it.'' To his credit, the other man sounded ill at ease with the tone of the conversation. ''It's up to Dante to put a stop to it if he doesn't like it.''

''Which he'll do only if he realizes the mistake he's making, and I'm not so sure he will. I rather think we're going to have to save him from himself, Johnny, my man.''

"Save him from himself? Uh...how?" Johnny, who-ever he was, sounded more nervous than ever. "Dante's treated me pretty well, Carl. Not that I don't appreciate having you in my corner and all, but I'd just as soon not give him reason to regret having taken me on when I needed a job."

"Relax. I've got a vested interest in keeping on his good side, too. We just have to be ready to run inter-ference when the opportunity presents itself, that's all. Which it will, sooner rather than later, and then you'll be where you belong—wearing the shoes she was never meant to fill."

"You seem pretty sure of that."

"I am. Drink up, pal, it's getting late. And mark my words. We won't have to put up with Lady Connors-Lee much longer. She'll be as stale as yesterday's news and just as forgettable once Dante's back on his home turf. Any affair that starts with a bang like this, practi-cally before the introductions are over, tends to burn itself out just as fast. In the meantime, a few well-placed words..." Newbury's voice faded as he heaved himself away from the railing and ambled back inside the room next door.

Long after the conversation ended and the door slammed behind the two men, Leila stood rooted to the spot, her face flaming. Oh, it was all very well to say that, compared to how she felt about Dante, what other people might think or say didn't count, but the plain fact was that it did. It hurt to learn that her reputation was being dragged through the mud, and it hurt even more realizing that Dante's was keeping it company.

And yet, hadn't she known all along that there would be talk in the ranks? Backing away from the window, she sank onto a wicker chaise, recalling her first meeting with him just three evenings before and the conjecture it had aroused.

She'd been among the last to come down to the cock-

tail party. Most of the other employees and their spouses
were gathered already in small, sociable groups, the
women in their elegant bare-backed dresses outshining
the flower arrangements, the men unusually formal in
bow ties and dinner jackets.

Yet for all that the wide flagged terrace held a near-
capacity crowd, he was the one who stood out from the
rest. On the horizon, a breathtaking sweep of jungle-clad
mountains soared to bare volcanic peaks. Between them
and the island, the setting sun cast a flaming swath on a
sea of rippled silk. But none of it could steal his thunder.

Close by, a woman had let out a subdued shriek of
dismay as someone accidentally spattered a drink down
the skirt of her dress. Offshore, a school of bottle-nosed
dolphins leaped in graceful arcs to the delight of the
audience on the terrace. Still, he'd continued to dominate
the scene.

She hadn't needed an introduction to know who he
was. Even in a crowd of sixty, there was no mistaking
Dante Rossi. He stood taller than the other men, larger
than life.

As if they knew he was different, special, his dinner
jacket clung more possessively to his shoulders, his
starched shirt gleamed whiter against the warm olive of
his skin.

He stood beside the balustrade separating the terrace
from the beach, engaged in conversation with Carl
Newbury, one of his vice presidents. But as Leila came
down the steps from the main house and attempted to
merge inconspicuously with everyone else, Dante had
lifted his head and lanced her with such a stare that she
stopped, as paralyzed as if she'd been caught in the act
of stealing the jewels hanging around the neck of the
woman standing nearest to her. And just like that, it had
begun.

With a dismissive gesture, he cut off Carl Newbury

in midsentence. Leila saw his mouth move, could almost lip-read his question *Who's she?*

The vice president turned to look. When he saw who it was his boss had expressed interest in, he allowed his face to settle into lines of holier-than-thou disapproval and mouthed, "That's her!"

Dante's observation had grown more acute, fastening on her features with an intensity from which she could not detach herself. But the hostility she braced herself to withstand hadn't materialized. Instead, another kind of awareness knifed through the atmosphere, strange, electric, thrilling. It rippled over her and whether or not she wished to, Leila found herself staring back at him, transfixed.

Where moments before she'd been surrounded by a blaze of color and movement and noise, suddenly Leila felt encased in silence and solitude. Carl Newbury melted into insignificance, too minor a player to merit notice. The women's gorgeous designer dresses paled. The animated buzz of conversation ebbed to the quiet murmur of waves lapping a distant shore.

In all the world there were only the two of them: Dante and she, potentially opposed from a professional standpoint, but at the same time, trapped in an inexplicable harmony that had nothing to do with business and everything to do with primitive sexual knowledge. A modern Adam and Eve, their association already poisoned by the serpent of resentment which had coiled around her from the moment she'd been hired to replace the ailing Mark Hasborough.

Dante had recovered first and moved, breaking the spell. Without taking his attention from her face, he lifted his right hand and snapped his fingers. A waiter bearing a tray of pineapple-garnished drinks had appeared at his side. Indicating to his vice president to take two glasses and follow, Dante had moved with sinuous grace among the throng of employees and spouses to where she waited. Carl Newbury minced along at his heels, as eager to corner her as a mongoose about to dispose of a snake.

"Dante," he'd bleated, rocking on the balls of his feet and smirking, "allow me to introduce Mark's replacement and the newest buyer to come on board at Classic Collections. This is—"

"Leila Connors-Lee." Dante's voice, as potent in its impact as everything else about him, had washed over her, eliminating Newbury in its undertow. He had unusual, beautiful eyes, their blue-green depths rivaling the clarity of fine aquamarines, and he had learned to use them to powerful effect. Framed in lush black lashes, they assessed her brazenly from head to toe, a cool sweep of appraisal that left her feeling stripped to the bone. "Of course," he said, relieving Newbury of both drinks and passing one to her. "You couldn't possibly be anyone else."

A more naive woman might have thought he was referring to the fact that she didn't fit the blond corporate wives' image, but Leila hadn't been fooled. He'd heard the gossip, the innuendos. Why else was he subjecting her to such thorough observation?

Vibrantly conscious of the electricity sparking between them and wreaking devastation on her composure, Leila had struggled to project an air of professional detachment. Refusing to crane her neck to meet his gaze, she'd addressed his mouth instead and murmured coolly, "How do you do, Mr. Rossi? I'm very honored to be here. Poinciana Island is beautiful."

In all fairness, he tried to match her aloofness. "We both know you're very *lucky* to be here," he corrected her, his handsome lips enunciating the word quite distinctly.

She'd lifted her chin a fraction. "You're referring, no doubt, to the fact that it's rare for such a very new member of the company to earn a place at its annual retreat."

"Among other things," he replied, taking her elbow and steering her toward a quiet corner where their conversation wouldn't be overheard.

None of the others had tried to join them but they noticed that he'd singled her out and they watched, some with slightly malicious anticipation and a few—mostly the women who'd befriended her—with sympathy and encouragement.

"So," he said, swirling his glass of rum punch and raising it in a brief salute, "how did you manage it?"

"What?" she'd replied, deciding two could play at being obtuse. "Getting myself hired by Classic Collections Limited?"

"We can begin with that, if you like."

He'd spoken as if it was immaterial to him how she answered; as if he didn't really give a rap who she was or how she'd managed to wheedle her way into this select gathering, and that he was merely going through the motions of pretending an interest in her.

But the tension in his tall frame had betrayed him for all that he lounged so casually against the terrace balustrade and declined to look at her, choosing instead to stare out to sea. Behind that veneer of indifference he was as conscious of her as was she of him.

The intense awareness that had sprung to life the moment their eyes met continued to writhe between them, its threat not *if* it would strike, but *when*. It left her heart pulsating unevenly and the palms of her hands clammy with foreboding.

But if some parts of her had shrunk from the danger of him, other parts had thrilled to it. Underneath her clothing, in places no man had ever seen let alone touched, her flesh grew warm and alive. For the first time in her life she had found herself in thrall to an attraction so uncontrollable, it left her breathless.

He was the most compelling, the most exciting man she'd ever met. That she should have leaped to such a

momentous conclusion in a matter of minutes had made
not a whit of difference. She simply *knew*, as surely as
she knew her own name. He was her destiny.

"I came across your company ad in a trade magazine
and decided to apply for the job," she'd said, somehow
managing to disguise her inner commotion with a calm
that was as superficial as the smile shaping her mouth.

"Why?"

Money and the debts she'd undertaken to honor were
too squalid a topic to mention when magic swirled in
the air. "Because," she said lightly, "it sounded interesting and I was ready for a change."

He favored her with a slow, engaging grin. "You
must also like a challenge. From what I understand,
you've not had much experience in the Canadian import
business."

"No," she admitted, warmed to the soul by his smile,
"but I'm willing to learn. I *do* speak Mandarin fluently,
and I'm intimately acquainted with the way business is
done in the Orient."

"Intimately?" He'd purred the word with such a
wealth of meaning that, fleetingly, she wondered if she'd
misread his interest in her. She knew that some of her
male colleagues, in particular Carl Newbury, believed it
had taken more than talent for her to come by her job.

"I was born and raised in Singapore and have traveled
extensively through the Far East," she'd said rather
stiffly. "How would *you* describe that?"

He'd brushed his fingers up her arm, the way one
might soothe a nervous animal. "What does it matter?
The important thing is, you made the move to
Vancouver and you're here now. Why did you, by the
way—leave Singapore, that is? It's a beautiful city."

"My mother wanted to return home after my father's
death."

"She's Canadian?"

"Yes."

"And your father?"

"Was half English and half Sri Lankan." But the pride she'd once taken in speaking about her father had been swallowed up in disappointment. As had become her habit since his death, she veered the conversation elsewhere. "Is there some point to all these personal questions?"

"I like to know about the people who work for me. If I'd been present at the time of your final interview, I'd have asked you then."

"Your partner seemed more than satisfied that I could handle the job, Mr. Rossi."

"He was obviously right. And the name, by the way, is Dante."

"But you're still not entirely sure he made the right decision in hiring me?"

His gaze had drifted over her again. "I wouldn't go that far. The simple fact is, I'm intrigued by you, Leila Connors-Lee. Women seldom perform so well on foreign assignments, especially not their first. They find the travel too demanding, intimidating even. Their ambitions lie closer to home as a rule."

He'd made ambition sound like a dirty word. "Is there something wrong with a person wanting to succeed?"

He'd shrugged, an elegant shifting of his shoulders beneath the exquisite Armani jacket. "The degree of wanting might be a problem."

"Why should it be, as long as the company benefits?"

"Theoretically, it shouldn't," he'd said, his glance taking inventory of the blush-pink Thai silk of her dress, the Sri Lankan sapphires at her ears, "but if other factors enter the picture...."

For a moment, her poise had almost shattered. Was he really telling her that he paid attention to the sort of innuendo Carl Newbury apparently was not above spreading around, or did a more subtle text underlie his words: one which acknowledged the sexual attraction pulsing between the two of them and, at the same time, that he rebelled against it?

"Other factors being the objections voiced by some of your executives at my appointment?" she'd said, and when he once again shrugged dismissively and turned away, went on, "Well, Mr. Rossi—Dante—I'd like to voice a few objections of my own, most specifically to your judging me on the strength of idle gossip. I know what's being said and I find it only a little less insulting than your willingness to accept as truth something which has absolutely no basis in fact. Frankly I expected a more enlightened attitude from a man of your presumed intelligence."

That had cured him of his urge to study the incoming tide! "The day I come to depend on the office grapevine in order to form an accurate assessment of *any* employee will be the day I retire from business," he said sharply, swinging back to face her. "I'm not sure who's been talking or what's been implied, Leila, but let's get one thing clear from the start. I consider myself a good enough judge of character to arrive at my own conclusions without relying on input from other people."

She'd been very firmly put in her place, no doubt about it, but before she could respond, one of the native Caribbean houseboys had appeared at the top of the steps leading into the house and banged a dinner gong. Its tones had rolled over the guests, cutting melodiously through the noise and laughter.

Barely able to contain his resentment at being excluded from his employer's conversation with the upstart newcomer, Carl Newbury didn't waste a second of the opportunity to intrude. Like a trained Rottweiler out to protect its master, he'd insinuated himself between her and Dante. "We should move inside, Dante. Nobody else is going to sit down to eat until you do," he'd brayed, all false amiability. "So sorry to interrupt your little chat with the boss, Leila."

''Don't be,'' she said, ignoring him and staring at Dante. ''Mr. Rossi and I have finished everything we have to say to each other, haven't we?''

Dante had flicked a minute speck of lint from his otherwise immaculate jacket cuff and shot her a glance from beneath the sweep of his lashes. ''Not quite, Leila,'' he'd said ambiguously, ''but it will have to do for now.''

The same dinner gong which had brought that first conversation to an end echoed through the old plantation house again, now summoning stragglers to that night's formal banquet and reminding her that almost an hour had passed since she'd stepped out of the shower. Dante would be waiting, wondering what was keeping her.

Yet how could she go down to meet him as planned, knowing that to do so would be adding fuel to the gossip already spreading like wildfire? He deserved better.

On the other hand, to remain in hiding suggested a guilt neither of them had reason to feel. They were consenting adults, free to pursue a relationship if they chose.

Granted, it would have been easier, wiser even, had they not been employer and employee. But love didn't acknowledge such trivial obstacles. Still, perhaps they should wait until they returned to Canada. Unlike Poinciana, the city of Vancouver was large enough that they could conduct their love affair away from the prying eyes that followed their every move here on this tiny island.

The sudden shrill of the telephone brought an end to her indecision. ''Leila, what's keeping you?'' Dante asked when she answered.

''I was...daydreaming,'' she said, for want of a better word.

''I've done a bit of that myself in the last hour or two.'' Even from a distance, his voice made her ache with longing to see him again, to be possessed by him.

"Hurry down, sweetheart. The cocktail hour's over and the banquet about to begin."

"I'm afraid I'll be a few more minutes," she said, searching through a drawer for fresh lingerie. "Don't wait for me."

"I'll keep a seat at the head table."

And set the tongues to wagging more furiously? "No!"

"Leila?" An edge decidedly more suited to a CEO sharpened his tone. "Is something wrong?"

"No," she repeated more moderately. "But singling me out that way will raise more than a few eyebrows."

"I can handle raised eyebrows."

"I'm not sure I can," she said. "Not quite yet."

"Our being seen together isn't hurting anyone, Leila. We've done nothing wrong."

"I know. It's just that I'm new here and...."

And there are some in the company who've made it pretty clear they think I'm prepared to sleep my way to the top. But if she told him that, he'd insist on names and he'd act on the information. And she'd got off to a bad enough start with some of her colleagues without making matters worse.

A moment of silence hummed along the line before Dante said, "Okay, we'll do it your way for now. Come down as soon as you can. If I can't sit next to you, at least let me be able to look at you."

"Of course," she said, her fears somewhat allayed.

Who was she going to listen to, after all: the man to whom she'd given herself in love and trust—or Carl Newbury and his misplaced moral indignation?

CHAPTER TWO

NEWBURY divided the dinner hour between shoveling food down his throat and harping on the fact that Leila had elected to sit at a table other than theirs.

"Glad to see you've managed to pry her off, Dante," he leered, swabbing a chunk of bread through the remains of his fish soup. "The way she gravitated toward you the first chance she got, I thought we were going to have to call in the troops to rescue you. It's no wonder the guys are up in arms about her. A woman like that can undermine the stability of the whole company."

"To put it mildly," Dante said, deliberately misunderstanding the last remark. Company be damned! In the space of a few days, she'd rocked the foundations of his entire life. Even now when he ought to have been occupied with other things, he couldn't keep his eyes—or his mind—off her.

She sat four tables removed from his, with her back toward him. Each time she turned her head to speak to the people seated beside her, the hurricane candle in the middle of her table illuminated her profile, emphasizing its exotic cast and highlighting the upswept coil of her black hair. She was the loveliest woman he'd ever seen.

"...Beginner's luck, that's all it is. Things just fell into place for her. That she should wind up enjoying a week here in the Caribbean when there are guys in the office who've been plugging away for years and never made it—"

She sat like a queen, dark-eyed, dark-haired, and so beautiful it was unnerving. Ethereal, almost. Like a dream that couldn't possibly live up to reality. Or was

21

it the blend of shy reserve and elegant dignity that lent such mystery to her? Or the fact that she seemed oblivious to her impact on those around her?

"Nobody bent the rules for her," Dante said, continuing to observe her. "The top thirty employees get invited to Poinciana, the rest stay and run things on the home front. The standard remains the same regardless of who's on the payroll."

"Ah!" Newbury pounced on the remark as eagerly as he attacked the stuffed land crab entrée placed before him. "It's the way she accomplished it, swanning in and taking over a plum assignment which was my right to assign, that soured me on her. But is she grateful? Not her! She treats me to the royal brush-off with her cool smile and snotty attitude. As if I'm not good enough to polish her shoes."

Considering Carl at times displayed all the charm of a sewer rat, her instincts were, in Dante's view, right on target. But the guy was married to Gavin's goddaughter, which made him family of a sort, and Dante set great store by family. So he kept his opinion to himself and hoped Carl would tire of the subject.

He didn't. "Her appointment's upset more than a few people, Dante. There's a discord present that wasn't there before she came on the scene. Knowing that, can you honestly sit there and tell me that, if you'd been there when she applied for Hasborough's job, you'd have agreed to hire her?"

No, he thought. *I'd have proposed to her instead before some other man beat me to it.* But the presumption behind Newbury's question was too blatant to go unchecked.

"Are you questioning the chairman of the board's business acumen, Carl?" He phrased the question pleasantly enough, toying idly with his wineglass the whole time, but Newbury heard the warning and took heed.

"Not at all! Gavin's a fine man—experienced, well respected in the import business. But he's.... "

"A pushover for a pretty face?" Dante laced his smile with phoney sympathy.

Newbury took the bait without a second's misgiving. "Well, aren't we all, Dante, if a woman plays up to us?"

"No," Dante said, his smile disappearing along with any semblance of congeniality. "Especially not Gavin Black and especially not where business is concerned. We're talking about a man who's already forgotten more about running an import company than you or I will ever learn, *and* who's a devoted husband, father and grandfather to boot. Yet unless I've misunderstood where all this talk is leading, you're suggesting he allowed his professional judgment to be swayed by what could well be interpreted as sexual discrimination."

"No!" Newbury practically choked in his haste to extricate himself from the hot seat. "I'm not saying that at all. Anything but!"

"That's good," Dante said. "Because if you were, Carl, I'd have to question very seriously if you really belong in a vice president's position."

"I worked hard to get where I am, Dante, you know that."

"And I applaud your dedication. However, I value loyalty more."

"So do I. The company always comes first." Newbury began to sweat.

It wasn't a pretty sight and reason enough for Dante to cast his gaze elsewhere. It zeroed in on Leila with the accuracy of a missile seeking its target.

Something the man on her left said had amused her. Dante watched, fascinated by the flash of her smile, the graceful arch of her throat as she tilted her head back in laughter. Everything about her was small, elegant, refined. Beside her he felt clumsy, unfinished. Too big, too earthy, too ordinary.

And he wanted her in a way that both startled and elated him.

As if she'd read his mind, she swiveled suddenly in her seat and stared at him expectantly. He realized then that she was not alone, that conversation throughout the room had died to allow one of the senior partners to give the annual morale-boosting spiel. This year, it was his turn.

Wrenching his mind back to business, he stood up and acknowledged the applause. "Thanks," he said, "and a belated welcome to Poinciana. We've already wrapped up two days of seminars and before the week is over I'm confident we'll have resolved some of the problems we've faced over the last year. But we don't fly our brightest and best to the Caribbean to spend all their time indoors."

Her eyes, dark gray and almond-shaped, fixed on him earnestly. Returning her gaze, he lost the thread of what he'd been saying, recalling instead the image of her lying beneath him that afternoon. His body responded accordingly.

In danger of finding himself seriously embarrassed in public, he looked away and scanned the room at large. "Classic Collections," he said, falling back on lines he'd repeated so often he could recite them in his sleep, "bought Poinciana five years ago but although it's the company name on the land title, the island really belongs to all of you. Your effort, your support, made its purchase possible. There are no bosses here and no employees, just people with a common interest and a common goal—to meet the challenges ahead with energy and a united effort to keep Classic Collections at the top where it belongs."

He indicated Gavin, his one-time mentor and for the last five years, his partner. "We hope," he said, and despite himself, found he was focusing on her again, speaking directly to her, "that you'll take advantage of the beaches, the trails, the weather and the excellent food, to recharge your batteries. Except for when you're in seminar, you're on island time. Make the most of it and enjoy.''

Right on cue the steel band on the terrace started its nightly gig, the rhythm pulsing through the applause in the dining room.

''Wonderful,'' Newbury murmured obsequiously in his ear. ''You always say exactly the right thing, Dante.''

''I try,'' he replied, stifling the inclination to tell the man to can it. Instead, he turned to Gavin's wife who sat on his other side. ''Shall we start things rolling, Rita?''

''Might as well,'' she said, smiling up at him. ''There are a lot of ladies who've waited all year to dance with you, Dante, and I wouldn't like to get trampled in the rush.''

Across the table, her husband laughed and held out his hand to Maureen Vickers, the fifty-six-year-old head of personnel who, like every other employee present, had gone the distance and then some in her devotion to the company over the last twelve months. ''Let's give them a run for their money, Maureen.''

The small dance floor filled quickly, forcing couples to spill out to the terrace. Above the coconut palms fringing the beach, the moon rose bright and full. The sea rolled ashore, seeming to be drawn as much by the hypnotic rhythm of the steel band as the pull of the tide.

A summer paradise beside which February in Vancouver sank into cold damp oblivion, it was Poinciana as he'd never seen it before, its beauty made all the more memorable because of Leila Connors-Lee. Automatically, his gaze swung over the crowd, seeking out her ivory-clad body swaying in the arms of a junior accountant whom Dante decided he'd never much liked. There was something about the man's soft white hands and the way they moved up and down that straight elegant spine....

"You're very quiet, Dante," Rita Black said. "Something on your mind?"

"No," he lied, spinning her around with more energy than style so that he could keep an eye on the accountant with the roving hands. "Suffering from jet lag, that's all. I got back from Italy only a couple of days before flying down here and seem to be caught in some sort of mid-Atlantic time warp."

"You work too hard, dear." Rita patted his arm sympathetically. "I sometimes wonder how you manage to stay abreast of things in the office, given the amount of time you spend on the road."

"It's as much a part of the job as making a point of dancing at least once with every woman in the room tonight." He steered her back to their table. "You'll forgive me, Rita, if I hand you over to Gavin now?"

"Of course." She smiled and waved him away. "Do your duty by the rest of the ladies waiting to take a spin around the floor with you, then sneak away. You deserve a little quiet time away from the spotlight once in a while."

And he intended to take it—although not alone.

Conscientiously, he danced with Meg, his super-efficient P.A., with the head warehouseman's pregnant wife, with a junior payroll clerk who was so nervous at finding herself boogying with the top brass that he thought she might wet herself.

Finally, as the moon slid down toward the horizon, he'd danced with every woman in the room except the one he most wanted to hold in his arms. Straightening his bow tie, he scanned the room, hunting her out.

Just as she'd known from the moment the music had begun that eventually he'd ask her to dance, so she knew to the moment when he decided the time had come. A sharp stab of expectation struck, puckering the skin of her bare shoulders mere seconds before he came up behind her, rested his hand lightly at her back and murmured with amused formality, "Would you care to dance, Ms. Connors-Lee?"

She inclined her head. "I'd be delighted, Mr. Rossi."

He led the way, threading between the tables to a spot where the polished wooden floor gave way to the tiled surface of the terrace beyond. She followed, aware as she had been all evening, of Carl Newbury's unremitting observation. How happy he must be that, at last, he had something worth watching!

Turning a deaf ear to the voice of caution that warned there'd be a price for the self-indulgence, she slipped into Dante's arms and let him draw her closer than was strictly proper.

"It's about time I had you back where you belong," he murmured.

But before they'd taken more than a step or two, the music stopped. Other dancers drifted apart, wandered back to their tables or chatted quietly with each other, and she knew she and Dante ought to do the same. Vice president Newbury wasn't alone in his scrutiny; they were all watching, those people who were his cronies and who thought she had no business being there, and she was fueling their resentment by remaining within the circle of Dante's arm, her gaze locked with his.

"I think we've left it too late," she said, reluctantly dropping her hand from his shoulder. "The band's packed it in for the night."

Refusing to let her go, he shook his head. "No. They'll play 'til dawn if we ask them to."

Then please let them start soon, she prayed, unable to slow her racing heart. Please distract me from losing myself in his eyes, from leaning into his strength and finding heaven in his arms here, in full view of such a judgmental audience.

The gods heard and responded kindly. The first bars of "Begin the Beguine" filled the night. Couples came together and picked up the rhythm. But Dante remained still, the message in his glance luring her ever deeper under his spell.

"Have you changed your mind about dancing?" she practically stammered, desperation threading her voice. Didn't he see the attention they were attracting? Couldn't he feel the curiosity, the undercurrents of hostility?

"Not in the least, Leila," he said.

She gave a little shrug to reassure herself that she still retained some measure of control over her body. "Then what are we waiting for?"

"Not a thing," he assured her, moving smoothly out of range of the watchers and into the tropical night. He drew her closer, steering her with a nudge of his thigh, directing her with the subtle pressure of his hand in the small of her back and, as the deep shadows at the edge of the terrace swallowed them up, inching his arm so far around her that she could feel the tips of his fingers brushing the side swell of her breast. "In fact," he murmured against her hair, "I think I've displayed amazing patience in waiting this long."

She didn't need to ask what he meant. She knew, and once again she marveled at the sense of rightness, of certainty, that swept over her, silencing her reservations. This was what her mother had been talking about the time she'd described meeting Leila's father.

"I knew the moment I set eyes on him," she'd said. "There was never the least doubt in my mind that he would be the love of my life. People were shocked, of course. I was the private governess to one of Singapore's most prominent families, expected to be respectable and, at forty-two, supposedly past the age to behave so recklessly. Falling in love with a man eight years younger, and of mixed racial origin, as well, created quite a scandal in those days, I can tell you, but that was a minor sin compared to my becoming pregnant within two months of meeting him.''

''How dreadful that must have been for you,'' the seventeen-year-old she'd been at the time had said. ''Were you terribly unhappy and embarrassed?''

Her mother had laughed. ''You've yet to give your heart or you wouldn't ask me that! When a woman loves a man as I loved your father, Leila, nothing they share makes her ashamed or afraid. Finding him was the best thing that ever happened to me. Having his baby was a miracle, a gift beyond price. If there is one wish I have for you, my darling daughter, it is that the right man will someday come along and fill your life with the same kind of happiness that I found with your father.''

''Even if I should be that lucky, how can I be sure I'll recognize him?'' Leila had asked doubtfully. ''How will I know he's the one?''

Her mother had touched a hand to her breast. ''You will know here,'' she'd said. ''And you will be as sure he is the one as you are that the sun will rise in the morning. He will *be* the sun in your morning, the moon in your night.''

Yes, Leila thought now, recognition binding her ever more securely to Dante with an inevitability that defied time or place or reason. That's it exactly! Now I understand.

The question was, did he? A sliver of uncertainty laid a chill over her bare shoulders.

Oh, he had made love to her with tenderness and passion, and he seemed not to care what others might make of their association. But when she had told him she loved him, he had not returned the sentiment. Was she naive to think that mattered? Didn't actions speak louder than words?

She looked up at him, seeking assurance that she wasn't in the grip of some self-indulgent fantasy. In the flame of the kerosene torches dotted among the palm trees, she saw the same awareness in his eyes, and heard it when he spoke.

"Perhaps I should have asked this before, Leila," he said, the words drifting over her face like a caress, "but there isn't anyone waiting for you back home in Vancouver, is there?"

"No," she told him, glad that she'd brought things to such a definitive end with Anthony Fletcher just before he left for Croatia well over two months ago. The one letter she'd received, a few weeks after his arrival in Europe, suggested he bore no scars from her rejection.

"No special man in your life?"

She shook her head. "No."

"There is now," he said, and this time the words touched her mouth a millisecond before his lips closed over hers to seal the promise.

Misgivings forgotten, she drowned in his kiss, reveled in the urgent straining of his body against hers. In the darkness of the balmy night, time stopped briefly and that other world, of ordinary people leading ordinary lives, faded into nothingness.

But not for long. Soon the steel band, the voices too close to go ignored, the hushed sigh of the surf rolling ashore, flowed over her, reminding her that, however much she wished it, she and Dante were not alone on this exquisite island. She remembered the suspicion of her associates which had dogged her from her first day at Classic Collections; worse still, she recalled the conversation she'd overheard only a few hours ago.

"Is this wise, Dante?" she whispered, pulling back and dispelling the enchantment with a stab at sound common sense.

"No," he said hoarsely, "but what the hell has wisdom to do with anything?"

It had to do with returning to the office when this magical week was over; with being able to stand proud and unashamed when he was away, conducting business on the other side of the world as he so frequently did, and she was left alone to face her critics.

She had come to Poinciana not just to learn more about the company but to show herself as a dedicated career woman, one deserving of the responsibilities inherent in her new job. Falling for the boss did not exactly strengthen her credibility in the eyes of those she was most anxious to impress.

Yet here she was regardless, helplessly in love with a man she hadn't known a week ago, and try though she might to negate the fact, it remained as fundamentally right as rain being wet or blood being red.

She could tell herself it was illogical, it was untenable, it was inexplicable. But the fact remained, it simply *was*. And to try to explain it was as pointless as telling a curious child the sky was up. There was no reasonable explanation.

Still, if she could not vindicate herself in the eyes of his employees, she could minimize the extent to which his reputation might be held up to scorn. Summoning up what little willpower she still retained, she said, "Anyone could see us here and if they do, they're bound to gossip."

"Let them," he said, trailing his hand down her throat, across her shoulder, down the length of her arm. "Let them," he said again, catching her fingers in his and drawing her down the steps at the end of the terrace, away from that other world.

Below, a path connecting the house proper to the beach found daytime shade under the scarlet poinciana trees for which the island was named. At night, their black umbrella shape cloaked the area in secrecy.

"Dante, wait," she whispered, slowing in their shadow. Her high heels were sinking in the sand, impeding her escape. Disappearing with him was ill-advised enough, without being caught in the act. "My shoes weren't designed for sprinting."

He stopped and knelt at her feet. Like a perfect gentleman he removed her sandals and set them aside. Like a perfect lover he lifted each of her feet in turn and kissed the instep. And then, without warning, he raised the hem of her dress and, cupping one of her calves in his other hand, he kissed her knees.

The erotic audacity of such a move started the tremors again, shooting them from the soles of her feet to end in shocking dampness between her thighs. She let out a soft whimper, half pleasure, half fear.

Murmuring reassurance, he pressed his face against her, and as naturally as she drew breath, she buried her fingers in his hair and held him to her, there where the quivering ache tormented her.

For long seconds he remained quite still and she suspected that he used the time to recoup control of himself because, when he finally rose to his feet again, though far from even, his breathing was less labored.

"What am I doing, sneaking into dark corners with you as if our being together is something shameful to be hidden away from the rest of the world?" he said huskily, standing a little apart from her as if he didn't entirely trust himself.

They were words she needed to hear. They gave her the courage to challenge the shoddy hypocrisy of men like Carl Newbury. "I am ashamed of nothing," she told Dante. "How could I be, when nothing in my life before this has ever felt so completely right?"

He groaned and pulled her back into his arms. "I'm not the type to rush blindly into a relationship," he said thickly.

"Nor am I," she said, but he made the mistake of brushing her mouth with his again, and the spark flared up anew, exposing their claims for the lies they were. How could she worry about the rest of the world, she wondered dazedly, when there was only the here and now. Only Dante Rossi and Leila Connors-Lee.

But then a shaft of light streamed from one of the upstairs rooms to pierce the shadows and she cringed. Instinctively, Dante swung around, protecting her from view. He loomed over her, a tall and dark presence except for his white dinner jacket which glowed like a beacon, advertising his presence to the people on the terrace.

Peeping over his shoulder, Leila saw that some guests had chosen to sit at the tables on the terrace the better to enjoy the balmy, flower-scented night. But their attention quickly focused on the figures suddenly floodlit beneath the trees, and the buzz of conversation dwindled into silence.

"What is it?" Dante said, at her little murmur of distress.

"They've seen us and I'm afraid they've recognized you."

His smile flashed briefly in the dark. "I certainly hope so!"

"But they'll talk and—"

"Yes, they will," he said, his tone serious "Does that bother you?"

She shrugged. "Yes. You...you don't need their disapproval."

"I'm the boss," he said. "I don't need their approval. I can do whatever I please, and it pleases me to be with you."

We're going to have to save him from himself.... Carl Newbury's threat continued to stalk her, for all that she thought she'd shaken it off.

"Dante, some of the men with whom you work the closest won't like that." She couched the warning as obliquely as she knew how.

She succeeded too well. "I don't blame them," he

replied, misunderstanding. "I wouldn't like it if one of them had laid prior claim to you."

"That's not what I mean," she said, scrabbling her bare toes in the sand to find her shoes. "They'll think—"

He cut her short. "Leila, I don't care what they think! All that concerns me is how you feel. Will it spoil your time here if I make no secret of the fact that I'm completely..." He drew a ragged breath and she froze, suspended on a fine edge of anticipation as he searched for the right word. "...Bewitched by you?"

How foolish she was to feel just a little let down. Did she really expect him to throw caution aside and profess he was in love with her?

Yes! Because she was in love with him, and whether that made sense or not didn't signify. She held no more sway over her heart than she did over the number of stars in the sky.

"Well, Leila?" he said, and she realized he was waiting for her answer. "Will it bother you?"

"I've never been a very public sort of person," she said, glad he couldn't see the disappointment in her eyes. Just because she was willing to accept love so quickly didn't mean that he was, and what, after all, was the rush? "I'd prefer it if, for now at least, we kept our...association private."

He stuffed his hands in his pockets and regarded her doubtfully as she bent and slipped on her sandals. "I'm not sure I'm a good enough actor to pull that off, but I'll try."

When the last strap was securely in place, he offered her his arm. Sedately walking her back up the steps and across the terrace to the dance floor, he waited until they were well within earshot of others before he said, "Shall we finish our dance, Miss Connors-Lee?"

Several people were there already, swaying to the rhythm as a native Caribbean in a snug-fitting white satin suit gave an impressive imitation of Belafonte singing "Scarlet Ribbons." She thought it would be easy to maintain the proper image and blend inconspicuously with the other couples. But the minute Dante took her in his arms, discretion melted in the tropical night. Imperceptibly he drew closer until he was holding her far closer than social convention allowed. And it seemed to her that everyone else noticed.

Sensing her discomfiture, he said, "Relax, sweetheart. We're only dancing. There's no sin in that."

"The way they're all staring, you might as well be making love to me," she said miserably, the blood surging in her cheeks.

He stroked his forefinger along her jaw, the smile tugging at his mouth belying the smoky passion in his eyes. "In a way I am. Or do you think I dance this way with every woman in the company?"

"I hope not," she sighed, temporarily dazzled into ignoring the ammunition they were giving Carl Newbury and his cohorts.

Common sense reasserted itself, however, as the evening drew to a close and Dante insisted on walking her to her room. The house, a restored sugar plantation mansion built at the end of the eighteenth century, was a magnificent example of neo-classical architecture, with tall pillars on the front of the building soaring to the tiled roof and separating the verandas lining the executive suites of the upper story. Inside, a wide staircase swept up from the great hall to a long gallery which branched off at each end to encompass two side wings.

Leila's room was situated toward the back of one of these, overlooking the lush rear gardens with their fountains and courtyards. "A good thing we're not next-door neighbors," Dante observed wryly, stepping aside as she opened her door. "The temptation to haul you over the veranda and into my bed would be too hard to resist." Checking first to make sure the hall was deserted, he dropped a swift kiss on her mouth. "Have breakfast with me in the morning?"

Although she hated to spoil the moment, conscience forced her to reiterate something he seemed wilfully determined to ignore. "Dante, you're asking for trouble. You haven't been around the office lately. You don't realize how—"

He kissed her again, lingering this time so that her words died on a sigh. "Make that an order, Ms. Connors-Lee," he murmured. "Have breakfast with me in the morning."

"Maybe." She closed her eyes, aching for him and knowing it would be professional suicide to give in to the yearning.

Perhaps he knew it, too, because the next moment he was striding away to the main gallery which housed the oceanfront executive suites, and she was able to slip into her room unnoticed.

At first he thought he'd be lying awake all night, his mind too filled with the tactile memory of her to allow him to rest. But three days of intensive seminars coupled with the previous month's overseas itinerary claimed him somewhere around one in the morning and dropped him into a black hole of sleep.

He awoke just after seven, feeling as if he'd been hit broadside across the head with a two-by-four, and with a restless dissatisfaction clouding his mind. Not exactly prime condition for a man who prided himself on always being in charge—of himself and of his company.

But the truth was, he hadn't been on top of things since that first night when she'd stepped out onto the terrace and stolen his...what? Heart—or sanity? Because the way he'd been acting was hotheaded to put it mildly, and atypical to say the least.

The only time he'd known anything remotely like this

had been during his senior year in high school when he'd dated Jane Perry.

"I love you," he'd foolishly told her, the steamed-up windows of his father's old Chev and his own rampant hormones driving him to indiscretion.

And for a few days, maybe even a week, he'd believed that he did. Certainly, it had been the right thing to say. Jane had become amazingly compliant and he'd been no different from any other boy his age when it came to experimenting with sex.

But the blush had worn off pretty damn fast when he'd cornered her at her locker between classes and said, "Hey, look, I can't make it to the movie on Friday."

"Why not?" She'd pouted, standing just close enough that the tips of her nipples had brushed against his chest.

"I've got a late basketball practice," he'd choked out, doggedly ignoring that part of him eagerly rising to the bait she'd so knowingly cast.

"Basketball?" Her indignation had bounced off the school walls. *"Basketball?"*

"Well, yeah. There's a big game coming up and the coach wants the team in top form."

"Oh, fine thing!" she'd snapped. "If you think I'm going to play second banana to basketball, Dante Rossi, you can think again."

"It's only for one night, for Pete's sake! This is important, Jane."

"And I'm not?"

"I didn't say that."

Her baby-blue eyes had welled with tears. "Prove it."

"Huh?" He'd been genuinely puzzled. Prove *what?*

"Prove that you really love me." She'd planted her fists on her hips and glared at him. "Make up your mind what you want—me or basketball."

Well, nice nipples or not, it had been no contest! "Okay," he'd said. "Basketball. So long, Jane. It was a blast while it lasted."

That had been it as far as he was concerned. Girls came and went but in those days, basketball was forever. End of love affair—or so he'd thought until Mrs. Perry showed up on his family's doorstep, weeping daughter in tow, and read the riot act at the callous way he'd behaved.

"You've broken my little girl's heart, Dante Rossi," she'd informed him and half the neighborhood, "not to mention sullied her good name."

Because he knew he hadn't behaved well, he'd refrained from pointing out that he wasn't the first to sample everything Jane was so willing to share, nor was he likely to be the last. Instead, he'd learned from the experience and never again made the mistake of confusing lust with love or indulged in a spur-of-the-moment declaration that he wasn't prepared to honor.

Instead he kept his feelings on a tight rein and if his hormones weren't always as firmly controlled, at least he made sure a woman understood the ground rules before she entered into a liaison with him.

After that, there'd been no room in his life for long-term commitment. His father and grandfather had earned a living making the best pasta in town for a company owned by other men. But good Italian son though he'd been, Dante had known he'd never follow in such mundane footsteps.

His priorities had followed a different blueprint, one in which success and personal fulfillment were built upon a foundation of pride and a determination not just to be as good as other successful men, but to be better, stronger, smarter and—ugly though some might find the word—*richer*. Because another lesson he'd learned well and early in life was that honest labor and pride in a job well done didn't, by themselves, guarantee the sort of success he was looking for.

It took more to inspire respect in a man's peers. It took power. Authority. And money.

Without money, a man never amounted to anything but someone else's patsy.

Until Leila, he'd found satisfaction enough in such a creed. Until Leila, he had scoffed at the kind of consuming romantic passion that afflicted other people and turned their ambitions toward suburbia and babies. Not that he didn't value family; it was probably his most sacred asset, the motivation that drove him to success. He just hadn't expected he was as susceptible as all those others. He was Dante Rossi, after all—king of his own corporate empire, too focused and too sophisticated to be blindsided by love.

He'd spent the better part of the last three days trying to convince himself of that—three days of covert glances, accidental touches that really were no accident at all, and flimsy excuses to strike up conversations with Leila in which the subtext of the words exchanged were charged with a powerful sexual innuendo.

And the result? Far from burning itself out, the attraction, the fascination—hell, the emotional involvement—had culminated in yesterday afternoon's interlude in which body and heart had come together to bend his mind in an entirely new direction.

As they made their way back down the trail to the plantation house after their lovemaking, he'd said, "I want you to meet my family," and waited for the familiar surge of caution to rise up. He never took women home; they seemed too inclined to view the move as the preface to a marriage proposal. He seldom even took them to his apartment.

"I'd like that," Leila had replied, and once again he'd waited. But all he'd felt was a wave of relief that she hadn't squashed the suggestion flat, then heard himself making plans for a future that went beyond the next few weeks.

For a guy who professed not to believe in it, he was

showing classic symptoms of a severe case of love at
first sight.

In his present frame of mind, he'd have been happy
idling away the day under a palm tree, with Leila beside
him and nothing but an occasional swim to distract him
from the pleasure of her company. Jeez! If any one of
his employees had come to him with such a lame excuse
for not putting in a full day's work, he'd have kicked
butt from here to Canada without a second thought!

Shoving aside the mosquito netting draped over the
bed, he staggered to the louvered doors, flung them fully
open and stepped out on the veranda, hoping a breath of
fresh morning air would restore his sanity.

From his vantage point, the reef protecting Poinciana
from the worst of the surf was clearly visible. Greenish
brown and shaped like a boomerang, it separated the
indigo blue of the open sea from the pale aquamarine of
the shallower water in the lagoon.

But that bright light glinting off the waves…!

He winced at the arrows of pain shooting behind his
eyes. The last time he'd suffered a headache like this
had been the morning after his brother-in-law's stag
night two years ago. Then he'd been hung over, plain
and simple. What ailed him now was anything but simple. In fact, it was damned complicated.

Given a choice, he'd have chosen to lay the blame on
the rum punch served the night before. At least that
wouldn't have cast doubts on his sanity. But knowing
the stuff packed a powerful wallop, he'd been very tem-
perate. Pity his restraint hadn't extended to his behavior!

Not that he cared for himself what anyone else
thought, but he'd picked up enough to realize that Leila
had already been put through the gossip mill. She hadn't
needed him to make matters worse.

Come to that, he hadn't needed it himself. He was a
man who liked to be in charge—of himself, of his sur-

roundings, of his fate. And suddenly, he found himself in control of none of them.

Unsuspecting of the chaos about to assault him, he'd looked up and seen her three nights before, and if he'd been poleaxed smack between the eyes, the impact could hardly have been more acute.

He remembered wading through the mob of guests toward her, helpless to prevent himself, yet hoping the whole time that closer inspection would reveal her to have the kind of flaws guaranteed to put him off any notion of furthering the acquaintance. Hoping she'd be so heavily made up that it would impossible to see the real woman underneath; that her voice would make a crow sound musical by comparison, that she'd be vacuous, silly, or best of all, married.

Instead, she'd been perfect. Lovely. Dignified and delicate. Intelligent and refined. As passionately drawn to him as he'd been to her and, by all accounts, not involved with another man. He'd wanted to fall down on his knees and thank God for the miracle of her. Before he'd even touched her, a bonding of souls had occurred from which he had neither the will nor the power to extricate himself.

He ran a hand over the stubble on his jaw. He supposed he should be grateful she'd had the wit to turn him down last night because if he'd had his way, she'd be lying in his bed right now and he'd probably be lying on top of her. Not a smart move for a man who prided himself on never mixing business with pleasure.

He needed to get his mind back where it belonged: on revving up the troops on the feasibility of setting up a base of operation in Argentina. A hot shower, a shave, and a pot of strong coffee should do the trick.

About to turn back into the room, he stopped, his attention snagged by the sight of a figure emerging from the house. It was Leila.

She crossed the terrace and stepped down to the

beach, her small footprints marking a trail through the freshly raked sand. Her swimsuit, a plain black one-piece thing, was modestly cut yet managed to define every curve, every hollow, every inch of her body. She'd tied back her hair so that it hung black and straight halfway to her waist. Her skin glowed apricot gold in the morning light.

She dropped her towel just above the high tide mark and waded into the water. When she stood waist deep, she waited a moment, perfectly silhouetted in the sunshine, then knifed below an incoming wave. Resurfacing another twenty feet out, she headed with smooth, easy strokes for a natural rock arch rising out of the sea at the eastern tip of the reef.

Dry-mouthed, he watched. And the fever to be with her came sweeping back, all the more compelling for its brief hiatus.

"To hell with business," he said, moving with a speed he'd have thought beyond him five minutes before and dragging on his swimming trunks. "Argentina can wait."

CHAPTER THREE

HER father had taught her to swim when she was only three years old and it had marked the beginning of a lifelong passion for her. Thoroughly at ease in the water, she'd spent many a happy hour with a mask and snorkel, exploring the secluded bays on the islands lying off the southwest tip of Singapore.

Although it lay farther north of the equator, Poinciana's warm tropical lagoon reminded her of those times. Even without a face mask she could see schools of fish darting among the coral heads below her: flamboyant striped angelfish similar to those of her homeland waters, gaudy Spanish hogfish, dramatic black-capped basslet and iridescent blue parrot fish.

More relaxed than at any other time since she'd arrived on the island, Leila lost herself in that quietly alive world. But the fish were shy, elusive creatures, posing no threat to her safety, so when something suddenly wound itself firmly around her ankle and held her immobilized, she almost screamed with fright.

Kicking herself free, she turned in a tight somersault and came up to find herself treading water next to Dante. Had it been anyone else, she'd have lambasted him for sneaking up on her like that. But how could any woman hang on to her annoyance when she found herself mesmerized by a pair of eyes made all the more remarkable by the color they stole from the sea and sky?

"I didn't mean to scare you," he said, cupping the back of her head in his hand and tugging her close. "I happened to see you leave the house and I just had to be with you."

He sounded almost indignant, as though he resented the impulses driving him. "But you wished you could have stayed away," she said, understanding exactly how he felt.

He nodded, the motion freeing the drops of water dazzling the tips of his lashes and sending them flying. Below the surface of the lagoon, his hips brushed against hers, a brief, erotic sweep of flesh against flesh. "Yes, and no. To be honest, I don't understand a thing of what's going on. All I know is that I've thought of precious little else but you from the moment I first set eyes on you."

Unable to resist, she slid her hands over the planes of his chest and up around his neck. "I know," she said. "It's the same for me. I could hardly sleep for thinking of you and when I did finally drop off—"

Inching closer, he smothered the rest of her confession in a kiss. Long and slow and full of sweet fire, it stole her breath away. And just like fire, it consumed her until she was nothing more than one pliant, aching flame that left her professional aspirations in ashes, along with sound judgment and any instinct she might once have possessed for self-preservation.

He pulled her into a tighter embrace, sliding his hands around her hips and molding her to him. Clinging together, they rode the gentle waves, oblivious to everything but the rhythm of their own passion. Caught in a current entirely of their own making, their legs tangled, mating with an intimacy that flooded her with a desire as overpowering as it was alarming.

What had happened to the woman whose signature trademark had always been the restraint and modesty with which she lived her life? Where had she gone? Until Dante, she'd never allowed a fully dressed man to take such brazen liberties.

Yet here he was now, practically naked and certainly making no secret of his arousal, twining around her with such potent effect that she was ready to offer herself to him without reservation, in full view of anyone who might happen to notice. To beg him to bury himself in her once again and ease the heavy, throbbing ache he'd awakened.

Before she could act on the impulse he pulled away from her, his eyes darkening with anger. "For Pete's sake, someone's watching us through binoculars from one of the front verandas!"

The blood, which seconds before had run rampant throughout her body, rushed to her face. "Oh, Dante, how mortifying!"

"I'd call it pathetic." Furiously he raked his hair back from his brow. "What the hell kind of nerve does it take for someone to pull a stunt like that?"

Backing away from him, she circled around until she was facing the shore. "Can you tell which room it is?"

"No. Whoever it was has gone back inside the house. But if I find out who—"

She was pretty sure she knew who. This was precisely the sort of action to which Carl Newbury would stoop. He'd justify it as—how had he phrased it?—"running interference...saving Dante from himself" and from a woman "willing to hand it to him on a plate."

"You won't," she said, starting back toward the beach. "The kind of person who resorts to voyeurism isn't likely to come forward and admit it."

Dante kept pace with her, slicing through the water in a side crawl which, for all its smooth execution, couldn't disguise the anger coursing through him. His expression, the sparking blue-green of his eyes, the compressed line of his mouth, painted a formidable portrait. In his present mood he was not a man to be crossed. "Well, I'm damned if I'll tolerate being spied on by my own people, though why anyone cares how I choose to spend my free time, or with whom, is beyond me."

It's not beyond me, she could have told him. Men like

Vice President Newbury didn't take kindly to a woman who parachuted over the heads of favored employees to grab a plum overseas assignment, especially if that same woman wasn't disposed to show a proper appreciation of her good fortune.

Should she tell Dante how unconscionably his vice president had behaved during those few days she'd spent in the office before she flew to the Far East for her buying trip? Would spelling out exactly what Newbury's idea of extending a welcome to the newcomer had entailed, help or hinder the present situation?

Had she and Dante not already become lovers, Leila would not have hesitated. But what she'd found with him—the unexpected, altogether miraculous meeting of heart, body and soul—was too new, too untried, to risk exposing it to the mud Newbury would sling around in a confrontation.

She'd heard firsthand his opinion of her, yesterday afternoon. But of what use was it to know that his hostility stemmed from her sharp reprimand just a few days after she'd been hired when he'd caught up with her in the library after everyone else had gone home for the day? It was unlikely he'd temper revenge with discretion if Dante called him to account on the matter. Hadn't he threatened as much?

"You're making a big mistake, doll," he'd said, when she recoiled at the way the hand he'd slung around her shoulder in a gesture of presumed camaraderie slithered to rest altogether too snugly around her waist. "I pack a lot of power around here and could steer some very nice perks a woman's way if she chose to cooperate. But in light of your unfriendly attitude…well, let's just say you'd better not get too comfortable behind Hasborough's desk because I can't see you warming his seat for very long."

"I don't take kindly to intimidation tactics, Mr. Newbury," she'd said coldly, any inclination to overlook the incident vanishing. "And if anyone should be worried, it's you. I believe there are laws in Canada protecting a person against the sort of harassment you're perpetrating."

"What harassment?" he'd said blandly, holding up both hands in mock bewilderment, and she'd noticed that his fingers were like uncooked sausages, short and pale and flaccid. The sight had made her shudder. "I'm just trying to be helpful to a rookie on the buying team, that's all."

"I don't need your kind of help," she'd said. "And if you ever lay a hand on me again, I'll make sure someone else is warming *your* seat in short order."

He'd shrugged and smiled. "It'd be your word against mine, doll," he'd sneered. "Sexual harassment cuts both ways and there are enough people around here already wondering what you had to do to land this job. You wouldn't be the first to try to sleep her way to the top and, as I said, I'm in a position of authority around here so, if it came to a showdown, who do you think would be believed?"

No, if Carl Newbury was confronted, he'd fall back on what he apparently did best and attempt to blacken her reputation in the eyes of the man who was now her lover as well as her employer. And the worst of it was, the way she'd flown in the face of social convention since meeting Dante would merely add credence to the story the vice president would undoubtedly choose to tell.

"I'll slip through the garden and around to the back of the house," she offered, as she and Dante waded ashore. "We'll attract less attention that way."

"No, you won't," he said grimly, picking up her towel and blotting the dripping ends of her hair. "Apart from the fact that it's a bit late for damage control, there's no way I'm allowing some sleazy Peeping Tom to dictate how you and I behave."

He seduced her all over again with those words. "We were probably asking for trouble," she said softly, "but I can't bring myself to regret a moment of what we've shared. Even if we could turn back the clock, I'd do the same thing again in a heartbeat"

His fingers tightened around hers. "You're sure?"

"Absolutely."

He stopped then, and stared deep into her eyes. The morning air was drenched with the scent of flowers. From the breakfast buffet set up under a long canvas awning on the terrace, the aroma of coffee lost its battle with the perfume of the red jasmine growing up the walls of the house. The sea whispered on the shore in concert with the faint clack of palm fronds shifting in the breeze. But they all paled beside the intensity that turned Dante's eyes the color of rare blue topaz, beside the heat of desire in his gaze as it scorched over her.

"I think," he said at last, "that I will have to marry you."

Her heart fluttered—with pleasure, with panic, with uncertainty. "Marry me?" she echoed.

Marriage was a major step, a union meant to last a lifetime. How could either of them make such a commitment after only four days? But the other side of the coin, the one that had led her to intimacy with a virtual stranger, stood firm, confident: this was the man she'd been born to love. How could she entertain a moment's doubt in the face of such certainty?

"I see no other solution," Dante said. "I have a company to run, family and social obligations to honor, and suddenly they mean nothing without you there to share them with me. How do you account for that, Leila Connors-Lee? What sort of spell have you cast on me?"

At a loss, she shook her head. How could she explain the unexplainable to him when it made no logical sense to her? They had met. It was as simple—and as complicated—as that. She had not been looking for love and she did not think he had, either. But her mother had been right all those years ago. Love wasn't bound by the laws that governed the rational world. It simply walked in uninvited and took over a person's life, regardless of whether or not the timing was convenient or appropriate or strictly according to protocol.

"Will you marry me, Leila?" Dante persisted in a low voice. "Or do you think I'm a fool to ask?"

She looked down at his hand clasped around hers. It was a strong hand, with the skin drawn taut over the sinew beneath, but its vigour lay less in its physical strength than in the spirit of its owner. She knew with a certainty that defied rational argument that this was a man who would not crumble in the face of adversity, who would not be coerced or pressured into taking the easy route out when life dealt unkindly with him. This was a man who would go toe-to-toe with the devil himself rather than submit to evil or wrongdoing, a man a woman could dare to love without reservation.

Still, "We met on Wednesday," she said, trying to be sensible for both of them, "and today is only Sunday."

"I have been waiting for you my entire life," was all he said, but it was enough.

"Yes," she said, her eyes misting over. "I feel that, too."

"Then you'll marry me?"

"Yes."

He bent his head then and kissed her in full view of everyone lined up for the breakfast buffet. No doubt they were all agog. A few would take pleasure in her happiness, some would be shocked, and Carl Newbury would be outraged. But none of it mattered. Because, as her mother had promised, she had found the man who was the sun in her morning, the moon in her night. What more could any woman ask?

Except for Carl Newbury who had business in New York and went there directly from the Caribbean, everyone else attending the seminar flew back to Vancouver the following Wednesday.

The volume of work needing attention at the office was such that, for the first couple of weeks after their return, people had no time to gossip. Eventually and inevitably, though, word of their romance leaked out and any thought she and Dante had entertained of keeping their liaison separate from their business lives was dashed.

On the evening of the last Friday in February, he took her to dinner at an Italian restaurant noted as much for its tastefully intimate decor as its excellent cuisine. A fire burned in the hearth of what had once been a grand Victorian parlor. Sterling silver and crystal sparkled against the rich burgundy table linens. Slender white tapers flickered amid a bouquet of pale freesia.

"I know we'd agreed to wait awhile before we went public with our plans," he said, as they waited for their main course to arrive, "but since we seem still to be the flavor of the month at Classic, I think we should let our families in on things before they hear about them from someone else."

"I suppose you're right," she said doubtfully. In truth, she'd cherished the privacy they'd enjoyed since coming home. The time alone together had enabled them to learn more about each other and cement the bond so quickly formed on Poinciana.

Dante reached for her hand. "You don't sound too sure. Are you concerned about how your mother and her cousin will react to the news?"

Leila smiled. "Hardly. Cleo told me before I left for the Caribbean that I would meet a tall, dark, handsome stranger who'd sweep me off my feet."

"Ah, yes," he said. "You did mention Cleo pretty well sets her clock by her Tarot cards. But what about your mother? You haven't told me much about her beyond the fact that she's been widowed for over a year. Is she likely to think we're nuts to be talking marriage on such short acquaintance?''

''No. My mother's been a rebel most of her life. Fifty years ago when all her friends were getting married, she wasn't considered sufficiently docile to attract a husband. It wasn't until she'd all but given up on the idea that, finally, she met a man who loved her for the way she was.''

''That was your father?''

''Yes. She found her niche, then, hosting posh soirees and cultivating the arts. But she never felt obliged to abide by the rules other people set down. She always did things on her own terms.''

Dante laughed. ''She sounds like a real character. I look forward to meeting her. But you're much more conservative. Do you take after your father?''

She hoped not. ''Some people think I resemble him in my quick grasp of languages and business sense, but I like to think I'm my own person.''

Dante was too perceptive by half. ''You don't much like talking about him, do you?''

''No,'' she said. ''Tell me more about your family, instead.'' She knew from earlier discussions that his parents were first generation Canadian, that his father's family was Italian, his mother's Russian, that Dante was the eldest of six children and all the rest were girls, and that his father, also, was dead. ''How long has your mother been widowed?''

''Sixteen years. I was twenty-one at the time.''

''And she never remarried?''

''No. I more or less became the man of the house, the one my mother and sisters turned to for advice.''

How would all these women feel about being supplanted in his affections by someone who was a stranger in every way, sharing none of their ethnic background and precious little of their Canadian culture, Leila wondered.

"Do you think your family will be pleased when you tell them?" she asked nervously.

"My sisters will be over the moon and my mother's likely to rush over to the church and light a candle to the patron saint of matrimony," Dante assured her, turning over her hand and pressing a kiss to the palm. "She's been praying for years that I'd give her more grandchildren—as if the eleven she's already got aren't enough!"

Children were another topic they'd discussed at length. "Well, sure," Dante had said, when she'd asked him if he wanted them. "Isn't that what marriage and family is all about?"

"Yes," she'd said. "But let's have more than one. Growing up an only child can be very lonely."

It was a comfort to know her future mother-in-law would approve on that score, at least.

"Before you've had time to learn all their names, my sisters will have you knee-deep in wedding plans," Dante promised, sensing her doubts hadn't been entirely put to rest. "Julia will drag out the lace veil that every Rossi bride has worn since my grandmother made an honest man out of my grandfather. Annie will want to bake the cake. Christine will try to shanghai you into letting all my nieces be flower girls. And the fact that we've decided to enjoy our engagement and wait until the summer to get married won't make a scrap of difference. They'll all still act as if everything has to be arranged by the middle of next week."

Just hearing about them was overwhelming. Leila had enjoyed a privileged childhood, looked after by a nanny when she was very young and taught at home by a governess until she was ten. After that she'd attended an exclusive private school and had never known the boisterous kind of family interaction Dante spoke of so fondly. Would she ever fit in? she wondered.

"Why don't we bite the bullet and set aside next weekend as 'meet the family' time?" Dante suggested. "I know, once you've met them, you'll feel better."

Still, despite his reassurances, she was more than a little nervous when, a week the following Sunday shortly before four in the afternoon, he parked his car in the driveway of the old three-story house where he and his sisters had grown up. It was not in a particularly fashionable district by present day standards but the garden was large and lovingly tended and there was a park next door with iron benches where families could sit and watch their children at play.

Pocketing the car keys, Dante turned to where she sat staring at the house. "Ready to face the firing squad, sweetheart?"

"I suppose so." She attempted a laugh. She knew that he'd already broken the news of his upcoming wedding plans. But despite his assurance that the announcement had been received exactly as he'd predicted, Leila's nerves were on edge. "It sounds ridiculous, I know, but my stomach's in an uproar."

The front door of the house opened then and, as if bent on testing her mettle, an assortment of children spilled down the steps and raced toward the car. Faces peered in the window, staring at her in unabashed curiosity.

"She's pretty," a pigtailed girl declared.

"She's old," a taller boy who might have been her brother decided in mild disgust. "She won't want to play football with us."

"She's here!" another child screamed, racing back toward the house. "Come and see, Mommy!"

Too soon Leila found herself standing on the driveway with bodies swarming around her. At her side, Dante perched a boy of about four on his shoulders and fended off another, perhaps a year older, who tried to climb his leg, while two girls grabbed at his knees.

On a tide of children and noise, she found herself swept up the front steps to the house and into a foyer overflowing with yet more people. The introductions seemed to go on forever though they probably took no more than five minutes. She survived the friendly scrutiny, even managed to smile and murmur hello. But the names...!

"You'll get us all sorted out eventually," a brother-in-law with movie star good looks said. He had a diaper draped over one shoulder and was burping a baby. "It took me a month before I knew who was who and I still get them mixed up once in a while."

"Because you're a slow learner, Charles," one of the sisters informed him affectionately. "I warned Stephanie not to be taken in by a pretty face, but she wouldn't listen."

"He teaches high school physics, in case you're wondering," another man told Leila as the group flowed down a narrow hall toward the back of the house. "He's probably the brainiest one of the lot of us, if truth be told."

In passing, Leila noticed a small, stiffly formal living room which had the look of a place seldom used, and a dining room similarly furnished. But at the end of the hall was a huge kitchen-cum-family room, a new and obviously expensive addition to the original house and clearly the favorite spot for family gatherings.

Copper pots and braids of garlic hung from an iron ceiling rack next to a massive range. Potted hyacinths filled the windowsill above the double porcelain sink. Custom cabinets lined the walls and formed the base of a center work island with a granite countertop.

At the other end of the room a fireplace alight with crackling logs gave off a pleasant whiff of wood smoke. Grouped around it was an assortment of overstuffed chairs and sofas covered in chintz. Toys overflowed from a wicker trunk and a battered old upright piano, its top filled with framed photographs, occupied space beside double French doors that led out to the back garden. Separating the working end of the room from the social area stood a long pine table set for dinner.

"The boys have dragged Dante outside to toss a football around but don't worry, he won't abandon you for long in these temperatures," the sister she thought might be Ellen told her, recognizing a lost soul when she saw one. "And this is nice because it gives us a chance to get acquainted without having the rowdies running wild the whole time. Leila, we were so thrilled when Mom told us the news."

"But he forgot to mention how tiny you are," another—Annie, Christine?—complained good-naturedly. "Even before the babies were born, my waist was never that small."

"You'll make a lovely bride," someone else announced, but it was Irene Rossi, Dante's mother, the only woman Leila could positively identify, who warmed her heart the most.

"And a beautiful daughter-in-law," she said, her smile and eyes so much like Dante's that there could be no doubt of the family connection. "My son has made me a happy woman today. I am proud to welcome you to our family, Leila."

They were all so warm and welcoming that she forgot she'd ever worried about meeting them. When Dante finally reappeared, he found her stirring the meat sauce on the stove and chatting with her future in-laws about the kind of wedding she wanted.

"That wasn't too painful, was it?" he asked as he drove her home that night.

"No," she sighed, so full of good pasta and home-baked fruit pie that she had to loosen the belt at her waist. "You have a wonderful family, Dante."

"Yes," he said, turning left from Cambie Street and heading along Forty-First Avenue toward the west side.

"There were times when we were growing up that I sometimes thought having sisters was a royal pain in the butt, but now that Mom's alone I'm glad there are so many of us. The neighborhood has changed since we were kids. The people who lived on the street when we were growing up have moved away or died and the ones who've replaced them are a different breed—working couples, mainly, with hardly any who are stay-at-home mothers baking their own bread or exchanging recipes over coffee. I don't know what Mom would do with her time if she didn't have reason to cook up a storm once a week or baby-sit the grandchildren at the drop of a hat, especially during the winter when she can't do much in the garden."

"I know what you mean. Cleo's a dear, but she's lived alone most of her life and has become something of a recluse. I'm afraid my mother's had a difficult time adjusting since we moved here."

"I'd never have guessed that, though I can see where she might find Vancouver a real backwater after the life she led in Singapore."

But the day before, when Leila had introduced him to her mother and he'd taken them to lunch in Stanley Park, had been different. His charm and the interest he'd taken in her life history had brought about a small miracle in Maeve Connors-Lee. For a little while the ghost of her old self had risen from its self-imposed exile.

Completely bowled over, she'd so far reverted to the witty, entertaining person she'd once been that lunch had lasted well into the afternoon. But while Dante and her mother had enjoyed the occasion, Leila had found it hard to reconcile the lively woman sitting across from her with the sad, withdrawn relic she too often found waiting when she came home from work.

"She did a good job of covering it up yesterday," she said, "but she's never really recovered from losing my father. After his death she couldn't bear to remain in Singapore. There were just too many reminders.''

''It's nice to hear of a couple still so much in love after nearly thirty years.''

''I suppose it is,'' Leila said, pretending an interest in the passing scene as the car travelled north along McDonald and turned onto Point Grey Road. She and Dante had shared so much about their lives but she didn't know if she'd ever be able to bring herself to speak openly about her father's suicide and the subsequent discovery that his debts so far outweighed his assets that nothing remained of the extravagant life-style he'd provided for his wife and daughter. Even after everything had been sold, some creditors still had not been paid.

Perhaps if he'd been a rogue Leila would have found it easier to talk about him, but until his death she'd always seen him as such a paragon of a man: decent, dependable and strong. Unfortunately, he'd made a bad decision in his choice of business partner and that one error in judgment had ended up costing him not just his material wealth but his honor, his pride, his self-respect. And so he'd ended things without thought for those he left behind.

At forty-two her mother would not have let such tragedy or circumstance defeat her, but at seventy-one she'd been too frail in body and spirit to start over in a city where, for so many years, she'd been known as a leading light of Singapore society and the wife of a highly respected businessman.

Instead she'd run—away from the headlines, the pity, the speculation—and back to the country where she'd been born and the only family she had left apart from her daughter.

Leila had chosen to come with her because, dearly though she'd cared for her father, at the end she had been ashamed of him. And angry and disappointed. He

had taken the coward's way out, leaving those he'd professed to love to clean up the mess, and it had almost
killed his widow.

Dante swung the car down the lane where Cleo's little
house, barely big enough for two, let alone three, sat
atop a small rise overlooking Georgia Strait. Parking in
the shade of the hawthorn hedge beside the front gate,
he leaned across the console between the seats and, pulling Leila toward him, kissed her, exploring her mouth
with as much wonder as if it were the first time.

As always when he touched her, the sweet, sultry
pulsing began, coiling through her blood, possessing her
limbs and clouding her mind to everything but the wonder of having found such a man to love.

The unhappy past slipped away, and all that mattered
was the magic of the present and the promise of tomorrow. Angling closer, she tried to shut out the space that
came between her and Dante. She wanted to feel all of
him next to her, his muscle imprinting itself against her
curves, his warmth filling her.

The pressure of his lips increased. His hand slid inside
the collar of her coat, caressed the length of her throat
and found her breast. She yearned toward him, the flare
of desire so urgent that it bordered on pain. With a little
whimper she covered his hand with hers and pressed his
palm against her sensitized nipple in an attempt to dull
the ache. It didn't help; she simply wanted him more.

She was not alone in her misery. "If I owned one of
those vans with smoked windows," he groaned against
her mouth, "I'd have you in the back with your clothes
off by now."

But he drove a low-slung, two-seater import, a Jaguar
whose only concession to seduction lay in its sleekly
beautiful design. And they were not, after all, teenagers
whose appetites so far outran their social conscience that
they could forget they were parked on a public street.

Reluctantly he drew back and smoothed her hair away from her neck. ''Will you miss me?'' he said.

She had tried not to think about tomorrow when he would fly out of Vancouver at dawn for four weeks of business meetings, first in London, then with clients in the Middle East and India, and finally with his Belgian and Dutch suppliers. But suddenly there was no more avoiding it.

''Terribly,'' she said, and thought how foolish she was to be near tears. What was four weeks when they had the rest of their lives to look forward to? And how could his leaving seem such a tragedy when, five weeks ago, she hadn't even known him?

''My sisters will be in touch,'' he said, cupping her chin in his hand and stroking her mouth with his thumb. ''Spend time getting to know them better. Take Maeve and Cleo to meet my mother. Go shopping for a wedding dress. Think about where you'd like to live, what sort of house you want. Keep busy and the time will fly by and I'll be back before you know it.''

Of course. Even though they didn't plan to be married until July, there was so much to do in addition to her work. Still, as she lingered until the last trace of the Jaguar's rear lights had disappeared and the subdued roar of its engine had faded in the night, she felt as if she had said goodbye to him forever.

CHAPTER FOUR

IF THE next two weeks were a living purgatory, they were at least made bearable for Leila by Dante's phone calls. Though nothing could make up for his actual presence or the feel of his arms around her, hearing his voice every few days went a long way toward keeping her spirits high, which was no mean feat considering the sort of harassment Carl Newbury took delight in leveling her way every chance he got.

She'd have preferred to have no dealings with the man at all but since he was vice president in charge of overseas buying, avoiding him wasn't possible. Once she'd compiled the inventory on merchandise already being shipped from Hong Kong, attached relevant photographs and a list of samples available for distribution to the network of sales agents across North America, he was the one to whom she presented her file. Her attempts to be brief and businesslike, however, were a wasted effort.

"What, still slumming around here now that you've hit pay dirt?" he'd inquired mockingly, lacing his stubby fingers over his midriff and regarding her with transparently insincere astonishment.

Refusing to dignify the insult with a reply, she'd slapped her report down in front of him and turned to leave. But he was quicker, moving out of his chair and around his desk with unsuspected agility and catching up with her just as she reached out to grasp the doorknob.

"You might think you've got the boss wrapped around your little finger," he whispered, "but I wouldn't count my chickens before they're hatched, if I were you.

Or, to coin yet another well-worn proverb, there's many a slip between cup and lip. Dante will come to his senses sooner or later and when he does....'' His snicker crawled over the nape of her neck, clammy and revolting as insect feet. ''...It'll be sayonara, doll, I guarantee you that.''

She longed to wipe the smirk off his face and tell him that she and Dante had already set a wedding date. But they'd agreed to wait until he came home before making the news public. So she'd swallowed her indignation and walked away.

Fortunately, her future in-laws were the perfect antidote to Newbury's particular brand of unpleasantness.

''Four months is no time at all to organize a wedding,'' they decreed, and besieged her with questions. ''Who do you want on the guest list, Leila? Where will you shop for your trousseau? How many bridesmaids? What color scheme? Which flowers? Which church? Have you chosen a china pattern, signed with a bridal registry at any of the big stores? No? Good heavens, how will people know what to buy if you don't draw up a list of the things you'd like? Do you really want to end up with five cappuccino makers, or six unmatched sterling silver place settings? And where would you like the reception to be held? The best places are booked at least a year in advance, you know.''

''I *didn't* know,'' she told her mother and Cleo, after one such marathon session. ''I had no idea planning a wedding could be so exhausting. I thought it'd be just a small, simple affair—we hardly know anyone here, after all—but Dante has such a large circle of friends and business acquaintances, as well as his family, that I suppose we can't avoid inviting a crowd.''

''How will we afford it?'' her mother worried. ''I'd love to give you a splashy wedding, Leila, but I don't know how we'd scrape up the cash.''

''That isn't your problem,'' Leila said. ''I'm not some

child bride with no realization of the sort of expense involved. These days, couples share the cost of getting married and, in a pinch, I can always sell some of my jewelery.''

As had happened with increasing frequency since the lunch with Dante, a flash of her mother's old spirit evinced itself. ''Out of the question,'' she proclaimed. ''We've been through this before, my darling, and I simply won't allow you to part with the only legacy your father left you. We'll find another way.''

Tossing her long gray braid over her shoulder, Cleo had rubbed her crystal ball and peered intently into its depths. ''All will be resolved,'' she decreed. ''Trust me.''

And so the first three weeks passed until finally only five more working days remained, and a weekend in which to polish her nails and tend to all those other feminine details that made a woman's reunion with her lover unforgettable. Then, after that, a Monday morning transformed from the mundane to the memorable by the knowledge that, at two that afternoon, his plane would touch down in Vancouver and she'd come fully alive again.

''Because since we've been apart I feel as if I'm floating somewhere between here and wherever he is,'' she explained to her mother, the Tuesday before he was due to return. ''I'm caught in a sort of jet lag. You're serving breakfast here but I'm miles away in my thoughts, sharing the sunset with him.''

Her mother laughed. ''So that's what's killed your morning appetite lately. I thought perhaps it was Cleo's cooking.''

''No, I'm the one at fault! Are all brides this self-involved, or is it just me, do you think?''

''You have a lot on your mind, darling. It's to be expected, given the changes that have occurred. Your life's taken a completely different direction, what with your new job and now Dante. You're not the same person anymore.''

"No, I'm not," Leila said thoughtfully. "I feel as if I'm living in a fairy tale."

But that evening, shortly after she came home from work, she received a phone call from Gloria Fletcher, the mother of the man she'd dated before she'd met Dante, which served as a pointed reminder that not everyone shared the same happy fate.

"Leila, my dear," Mrs. Fletcher stammered, "we've just received word. There's been a terrible accident—an explosion—in Croatia. And Anthony... '' Her voice broke, a signal in itself that the news was bad. No part of Gloria Fletcher broke easily; she had a will of iron.

Leila's heart contracted with dread. An image of Anthony as she'd last seen him, tall, proud and sleekly handsome, filled her mind. It hadn't been a particularly happy occasion. Telling him she did not love him and that she saw no future for them as a couple had not been easy. Still, she was fond of him and considered him a good friend—indeed, one of the few she had in Canada. The one or two letters she'd received from him since suggested he'd accepted her decision and harbored no ill feelings, and the thought of him lying half a world away, maimed, scarred, or worse, shocked her immeasurably.

"Oh, Mrs. Fletcher," she breathed. "You're not saying...?''

"He suffered a serious head wound, a fractured skull we believe, but mercifully is now out of danger.'' A sharp inhalation from the other end of the line was indication enough that Anthony's mother had recovered her usual fortitude. "We won't, of course, know the full extent of his injuries until we see him. He's been hospitalized in Germany for the last two weeks and only just managed to get word to us. Thank God he's recovered enough to be flown to Vancouver the day after tomorrow.''

"I'm so terribly sorry," Leila said. "What a shock for you and your husband."

"And for you, my dear. I gather you had no idea that anything was amiss?"

It struck Leila as an odd question, given the fact that there'd been so little communication between her and Anthony during what now amounted to the more than four months he'd been gone. Didn't his family know they'd parted as friends, not lovers? "No idea at all," she said.

"Well, you have now and we know you'll want to be there for him when he arrives home. His flight arrives at eleven on Thursday morning and although I realize you're normally working at that hour, I'm sure your employer will allow you to take the day off, considering the circumstances."

"That's very kind of you, Mrs. Fletcher, but I'd feel like an interloper. Given Anthony's condition, this is surely a private family time."

"We consider you practically part of the family, my dear."

There it was again, another unsettling suggestion that her romance with Anthony was still in full flower. Searching for a tactful way to set the record straight, Leila said, "Still, the flight from Europe is tiring even to someone in the best of health. Why don't you call me once you see how he's feeling? He might not be up to seeing anyone for the first few days."

"He'll want to see you," Mrs. Fletcher declared with more than a trace of impatience. "We spoke to him briefly on the telephone just before I called you, and he was very clear about that. You won't disappoint him, Leila, I know."

Less a question than an order clothed in Mrs. Fletcher's cultured velvet tones, it was impossible to refuse without sounding churlish or insensitive.

And perhaps, Leila thought, it was best this way. She

could well spare a morning away from the office. She'd attended to most of the paperwork and numerous follow-up details required to ensure smooth delivery of the goods she'd purchased in the Far East. All that remained was to catalog her sources for future reference, something she could easily do by working late one evening.

It seemed more urgent that the misapprehension Anthony's parents entertained regarding her relationship with their son be cleared up, especially in light of the fact that she was now unofficially engaged to another man. But it was hardly something to blurt out over the phone, especially not at a time like this.

"Leila? Are you still there?" The well-bred voice held a decided edge this time.

"Yes, Mrs. Fletcher."

"Then it's arranged? We'll see you on Thursday?"

"I'll be there," she said.

"I knew we could count on you, my dear. Anthony needs you now more than ever."

The confidence with which the words were uttered did nothing to alleviate the sense of foreboding lodged uncomfortably in Leila's stomach and which no amount of rationalizing could dispel.

It was just as well Dante would be home within the next week, she thought. The sooner their engagement became public knowledge, the better.

It helped, having friends in high places, Dante decided, racing along the concourse at Schiphol on Thursday evening. Otherwise, he'd have been cooling his heels another night in Amsterdam. As it was, a phone call and a generous tip in the right hands had been enough to guarantee him the last available seat on the flight to Toronto that night.

A clock on the wall showed thirteen minutes to eight. Less than ten minutes to clear security and reach the gate where the crew of the 747 jet would be preparing for final clearance prior to departure. They'd wait for him, of course; he'd made sure of that. But they wouldn't be happy. Businessmen who used their executive clout to hold up international travel were never popular. Not that he made it a practice to keep a loaded aircraft waiting on his whim and he didn't expect his fellow passengers to greet him with a round of applause. But they didn't have a woman like Leila waiting on the other end. Perhaps if they had, they'd view him more sympathetically.

Patting the breast pocket of his jacket where he'd stashed the diamond ring he'd bought that morning, he hoisted his briefcase over the head of a young mother wheeling a baby stroller and dodged around a group of Japanese tourists huddled around the entrance to the duty-free shop. Five minutes later he was sprinting down the last stretch and into the already deserted departure lounge.

"Sorry," he panted, handing the waiting flight attendant his ticket and drumming up his most winning smile. "I know I'm cutting it fine."

She pursed her lips and muttered something unflattering. He shrugged another apology and headed down the boarding ramp with her breathing fire at his back. So what if they fed him bread and water while the others in business class dined on caviar, lobster and champagne? He could survive almost anything but being apart from Leila a minute longer than he had to be. It was what had motivated him to cram six days of business into two and made it possible for him to fly home four days earlier than originally planned, although he hadn't known until that morning if he was going to pull it off.

Sliding his briefcase into the overhead bin, he buckled himself into his seat seconds before the aircraft gave a slight jerk and eased away from its berth. Taking into account the time change and the one hour stopover in Toronto, he'd land in Vancouver at a quarter past midnight. Even if the flight was on time, it'd be a bit too late to call Leila and let her know he was back, but surprising her when she walked into the office the next morning would more than make up for that.

He leaned his head back and closed his eyes, savoring the sense of completion she brought to his life and wondering how he'd find the patience to wait another four months before he married her.

It was over, the whole horrifying, upsetting day. Emotionally wrung out and sick to her stomach, Leila let herself into the house shortly after eight on Thursday night. How was she going to extricate herself gracefully from a situation whose complications no one could possibly have anticipated?

Her mother appeared in the kitchen doorway. "Leila? We've saved dinner for you and it—good gracious! Darling, you look dreadful. Are you ill?"

Actually, she hadn't felt well for the past couple of days but it was nothing she could put her finger on. Just a nagging sort of malaise which left her feeling tired and generally out of sorts and which she'd put down to stress. And heaven knew today's events had been enough to turn the most stalwart individual a little green around the gills.

"Not exactly. Just very tired and shocked." She hung up her coat in the hall closet and leaned against the door.

Wiping her hands on her apron, her mother drew her into the dining room where a fire burned in the hearth. "Is it Anthony, darling? Are his injuries much worse than you'd expected? You look... " Perplexed, Maeve lifted her shoulders and turned to her cousin. "Well, shell-shocked is the term that comes to mind, wouldn't you say, Cleo?"

Leila sighed. "That just about sums it up for Anthony, Mother, I'm afraid."

"You need a good stiff drink, darling," her mother said, pressing her into a chair and reaching for the sherry bottle on the sideboard.

But it would take a lot more than Harveys Bristol Cream to erase the memory of seeing Anthony again, Leila thought. Nothing she'd been told had prepared her for the slumped figure in the wheelchair, the haggard face or the vacant expression in the eyes of the man who had been a Rhodes scholar and a star athlete during his university years.

Only when he'd caught sight of her standing beside his parents had his face lit up in a smile and chased away the frightening emptiness in his eyes. "I knew you'd be here, my love," he'd whispered, taking her hand and clinging to it. "I knew you would."

She'd felt the tears streaming down her face. Finding him so frail and helpless had been a heart-wrenching experience made more unbearable by the flashbulbs exploding around them as the press and local news crews captured the moment for their audiences.

Of course, she should have expected that. The Fletchers were a high-profile family, one of the wealthiest and most prominent in the province, let alone the city. The simple fact of their stepping outside the grounds of their home was reason enough to bring the media running. But she had not foreseen finding herself caught in the spotlight.

Mr. Fletcher, on the other hand, had come prepared. When asked for a statement, he'd tugged the lapels of his Burberry coat firmly into place and brought his emotions under control with equal dispatch. "Our son has come home a hero," he said. "His mother and I are very proud of him and deeply grateful that he has been spared." He had turned and nodded to where Anthony still clutched Leila's hand. Bathing the pair of them in a smile, he finished, "As you can see, he has a great deal to live for and we all know there's nothing like the love of a good woman to speed a man to recovery.''

"So there I was, Mother," Leila explained, "left with my mouth more or less hanging open and nothing coming out to set the record straight.''

"But you ended the relationship weeks before Anthony left for eastern Europe!" her mother exclaimed, while Cleo clucked dolefully and poured herself a generous shot of sherry.

"But he doesn't remember," Leila said. "That's the whole trouble. He's suffering from some sort of neurological trauma inducing episodic amnesia and seems to be under the impression that we're still a couple.''

"But you're not, darling! You're engaged to Dante. You've set a wedding date.''

"Exactly." Leila took a sip of the sherry and felt her stomach rise in revolt. "But try telling that to a family whose son is still recovering from a serious brain injury and who doesn't need anything to bring on a setback. He looks like hell, Mother. He's lost weight, his eyes are sunken, his head's been shaved except for a patch of hair at the back, and he can't even walk without assistance because his sense of balance is affected.''

"Your language has gone to the dogs since you moved here," Cleo remarked virtuously.

"I'm not trying to be intentionally offensive, Cleo. Quite frankly, the shape he's in right now, Anthony might well have just come back from hell.''

"You don't look all that much better yourself," her mother observed. "When did you last eat?''

"I can't remember. One of the Fletcher maids set up a buffet in the dining room but I wasn't hungry. No one was, really, although we went through gallons of coffee." Leila raised her sherry glass to her lips but the smell of the normally pleasant aperitif struck a markedly offensive note. "Maybe that's what's given me an upset stomach," she said, putting the glass aside.

"You complained of the same thing this morning, too, my darling, before you'd touched a thing. And you weren't feeling too swift the morning before that, either."

"I miss Dante. Once he's back, I'll recover my appetite."

"Don't be too sure of that," Cleo muttered, poring over the cards she'd laid out on the table.

"Well, what other reason could there be?" Leila swallowed, trying to relieve the faint but persistent queasiness. "In any case, I'm sure it's nothing a good night's sleep won't fix."

But she was hardly out of bed the next morning before the nausea attacked again, this time so potently that she barely made it to the bathroom in time. "My goodness," she said weakly, accepting the cold washcloth her mother handed to her and mopping her face. "It must be the flu."

"You think so, do you?" Cleo said from the doorway. "How long have you and Dante known each other, sweet innocent?"

"Just over eight weeks."

"And is it impertinent of me to assume you have made love during that time?"

"Not for the last four weeks. He's been away."

"But before that? You were intimate?"

Being twenty-nine didn't protect a person from blushing in the face of such outspoken curiosity, Leila discovered. "We're consenting adults, Cleo."

"With normal healthy appetites, I don't doubt."

"That's one way of putting it, I suppose."

"Indeed." Cleo tugged the belt of her dressing gown more tightly around her waist and came to perch on the edge of the bathtub. "And as consenting *informed* adults, you naturally used a condom?"

"Cleo!" Maeve gasped, appalled. But her expression

mirrored Cleo's question and she quavered, "Did you, Leila? Take…precautions, that is?"

"Once we came home from Poinciana we did, yes. Of course."

"But before that?"

Leila didn't like the direction in which her relatives' questions were leading. "Not the first time or two. We hadn't exactly planned in advance to fall in love and the island isn't littered with drugstores conveniently stocked with contraceptives. But if you're suggesting I might be pregnant—"

She broke off as another attack took hold. "I'm not pregnant," she insisted, when the spasm passed.

"That's what they all say," Cleo intoned.

"She's right," Maeve said. "When morning sickness struck me, I continued to deny it for months, but it didn't make a bit of difference. You were born the following summer, regardless. Maybe you should forget about going to work today, Leila, and make an appointment to see a doctor instead. Because, if you *are* pregnant—"

"She is," Cleo declared smugly.

"—Then you can't afford to wait four months to get married. You'll need a bouquet as big as a house to hide your condition."

"I'll get the car out," Cleo said, referring to the ancient Chevrolet she drove on average twice a year. "Maybe when a so-called expert confirms what I already know, you won't be so quick to scoff at my powers."

He'd come in to the office early. Before seven. Before anyone else, even the warehouse crew, was on the scene. Fool that he was, he'd thought to surprise her. He'd left an orchid on her desk. It would've been the first thing she'd seen when she walked through the door and she'd have known at once that it was from him; that he'd shaved four days off his itinerary just to be with her, to

ease the loneliness that she'd claimed had laid her low
every minute she was apart from him.

Instead, he was the one who'd been surprised.

Surprised? Hell, ambushed was more like it! And
nothing to cushion the blow but the photograph of her
spread across the front page of that morning's edition of
the city's biggest daily newspaper which Carl Newbury
had so thoughtfully brought to his attention the minute
he'd learned he was back behind his desk.

"I did try to warn you, pal, remember?" Newbury
said, the commiseration in his voice woefully negated
by the glee in his eyes as he waited for Dante's reaction.
"The night of the banquet on Poinciana, I did my
damnedest to make you see the kind of woman she is,
but you didn't want to hear."

"I don't now," he'd said, still nursing the futile hope
that at any moment she'd appear at the door and offer a
perfectly reasonable explanation for the camera having
caught her in a clinch with the heir to the Fletcher empire.

"I suspected all along she was a tire-biter, Dante, and
from the looks of it, she's proved me right. Sorry to have
to be the one to say it, but what you've got to offer
doesn't amount to a hill of beans beside what Anthony
Fletcher can give her."

An indisputable if unpalatable truth! Dante made a
pretty good living, enough to set his mother up in something approaching the style she deserved. Enough to
make sure that his sisters' families didn't want for anything. Enough that he could live pretty high on the hog
with his penthouse and imported car and holidays just
about anywhere on the globe he cared to go. But Carl
was right: it all added up to small change compared to
the Fletcher fortune.

Not that he needed Newbury or any other so-called
concerned friend planting ugly suspicions in his mind.
He was doing a good enough job of that all by himself.

So he'd sent Newbury on his way with a curt reminder that he wasn't being paid to theorize on matters about which he knew less than nothing, and he'd waited. Nine o'clock had come and gone. Ten had rolled around. Ten-thirty.

The slow-burning rage ran amok then. Because no matter how much he'd have preferred to believe otherwise, there was no changing the fact that her nonappearance went beyond mere tardiness. The orchid, the surprise return, the certainty with which he'd sailed into the building at dawn had been for nothing. She wasn't going to show, period.

He wasn't used to sitting back and waiting for things to happen. He'd been a take-charge type from the word go—"bossy" was the word his sisters had used when they were kids—and he wasn't about to change the habits of a lifetime now. He wanted answers. Damn her, she owed him that much, at least.

Yanking the phone toward him, he'd punched in her home number. No answer, just the ongoing monotonous peal of the bell that, from the first, somehow conveyed the emptiness of the house at the other end. Still, he let it ring fifteen times. Because even if she wasn't there, where in hell was her mother or the cousin? Unless....

Just briefly the rage faltered. Could there have been an accident?

Then his glance fell on the newspaper again, on the article accompanying the photo and the words he didn't want to acknowledge. "... still suffering from wounds suffered in bridge explosion, prominent industrial magnate's son returns home a hero...flanked by family and longtime love Leila Connors-Lee. When asked if there'd be wedding bells in the near future, a smiling Samuel Fletcher told reporters, 'My son's full recovery is obviously the first order of business, but after that? Well, let's just say we have nothing but good things to look forward to.'"

Oh, there'd been an accident all right but Dante Rossi was the victim! He'd behaved as recklessly as a teenager behind the wheel of his first fast car. He'd mixed business with pleasure, and left himself open to being made the laughingstock of everyone who'd witnessed his infatuation on Poinciana.

"Son of a bitch!" With a backhanded swipe of his fist, he sent his in-basket flying, indiscriminately spewing four weeks of memos and mail across the carpet.

In less time than he usually took to sign a business contract, he'd asked a stranger to marry him, an aberration he could only ascribe to some sort of rare tropical fever. The real pity of it, though, was not that he'd succumbed so easily but that his recovery had not manifested itself sooner—before he'd dragged his family into the whole ridiculous farce.

He knew they'd be waiting for explanations, that they'd look to him to clear up the mess. And he would, just as he always did. But not yet. Not until he could trust himself to be utterly in control. Not until he could be sure the rage wouldn't sneak up and betray him. He'd rather be dead than let anyone know that his pride had taken such a beating.

Because that's all it was: embarrassment for having subjected himself to the indignity of acting like a fool in front of witnesses. The howling emptiness echoing inside him had not one good goddamned thing to do with love. Hell, how could it have? Of the eight or nine weeks he'd known her, they'd spent less than half together.

That didn't add up to love; there was another name for it entirely.

The Fletchers of the world, with their pedigrees and fraternity rings, would call her an amusing diversion but he was the son of common working people. Immigrants who'd slaved by the sweat of their brow. Plain-living, plain-speaking folk not given to varnishing the truth, because that didn't put bread on the table or shoes on the kids. Following along in that tradition, he'd call her what she was: a good lay. And for him to have confused that with love showed him as nothing but a fool. He needed a couple of days to come to terms with that.

But first, there was business to attend to. He hadn't slaved the last eight years to make Classic Collections the success it was today, just to flush it all down the tubes because of an affair gone sour.

Reaching for the phone again, he called up his assistant on the intercom. "I'm not here, if anyone asks, Meg," he said. "If anyone calls, you haven't heard a word since I faxed you from Brussels two days ago and you don't know exactly when I'll be back in the office."

He didn't lift his head again until after six o'clock that night, but by then he'd dealt with every last item requiring his attention. Yet through it all, thoughts of her kept running through his mind.

What if she were ill? Or her mother—or the flaky cousin? Could there be a reasonable explanation for the morning paper's article?

Wearily, he rubbed his aching eyes and flicked on the TV news station just as the stock market report was winding up. "And now for the latest on Anthony Fletcher," the announcer began, and as if the written word hadn't been proof enough, the screen showed in full living color yesterday's scene at the airport.

"Today," the news anchor continued, "Fletcher is home and sufficiently recovered to receive visitors."

The picture changed to reveal the Fletcher estate, walled to keep out the gawking public. But the woman climbing out of the car which the armed security guard had allowed past the gate was instantly recognizable. Dante saw her quite clearly, being embraced by Mrs. Samuel Fletcher and ushered into the house.

So, she wasn't ill; wasn't flat on her back with two broken legs. Wasn't anything, in fact, but exactly what Newbury had described her being: a social-climbing gold digger who'd dumped him for someone who could give her a richer life.

Well, to hell with her!

Lunging out of his chair, he strode from the room, leaving the TV weatherman blatting on about spring being just over the horizon.

An hour and fifteen minutes later, he was en route for Whistler-Blackcomb and a weekend of taking on the worst the ski resort could offer in the way of death-defying challenge. Because nothing got the best of Dante Rossi. Not a mountain, not a millionaire, and most certainly not a woman!

CHAPTER FIVE

MORNING sickness played havoc with punctuality. Leila was late to work on Monday, arriving shortly after nine o'clock, a full half hour past her usual time.

Gail Watts, the secretary she shared with two other overseas buyers, intercepted her on her way in and handed her a sheaf of message slips. "We missed you on Friday, Leila."

She'd had too much on her mind that day to think about the inconvenience her absence might have caused. "I'm sorry," she said, sticking as close to the truth as possible. "I wasn't feeling well, but that's no excuse for not phoning to let you know I wouldn't be in. Is there anything I missed that needs attending to right away?"

She hoped there wasn't. The soda crackers and weak tea she'd consumed before leaving the house didn't seem particularly anxious to prolong their acquaintance with her.

"Nothing so urgent you needed to kill yourself getting here." Gail tipped her head to one side and inspected her sympathetically. "You still don't look so hot. Are you sure you shouldn't be home in bed?"

Swallowing the nausea clogging her throat, Leila attempted a smile. "Give me a few minutes to get caught up and I'll be fine."

"Sure. Would coffee help?"

Dr. Margaret Dearborn, the obstetrician she'd seen on Friday afternoon, had assured Leila morning sickness was generally considered the sign of a well-implanted embryo and an inconvenience that normally lasted only for the first trimester, but she'd neglected to explain how thoroughly it could monopolize a person's life during that time. The mere thought of coffee almost undid Leila.

"No, thanks," she said, and sat down before she fell down. Someone, she noted peripherally, had left a faded orchid on her desk.

Gail nodded. "Okay. Give me a shout if you change your mind. Oh, by the way, the boss is back, in case you hadn't heard."

"Dante's back? Are you sure? I wasn't expecting him until later this afternoon."

"Saw him with my own eyes not fifteen minutes ago."

Delight achieved what soda crackers could not; temporarily at least, the nausea subsided. "Oh, that's wonderful!"

"Amazing what a little good news can do for a woman's state of health," Gail remarked, dropping a sly wink.

"Isn't it just! Take a message if anyone calls me in the next half hour, will you? I'll be tied up in a meeting that can't be put off a minute longer!" Already halfway to the door, Leila stopped suddenly and spun around. "Gail, do I really look washed out?"

"You no longer look like something the dog just dug up, if that's what you mean, but a little blusher wouldn't hurt."

It was as she left the ladies' room after acting on Gail's advice that Leila ran into Carl Newbury, and something about his expression—a hint of malicious satisfaction—set her stomach to quivering unpleasantly again.

Doing her best to ignore the way his gaze roamed over her, she continued down the hall to the corporate wing. Dante's assistant was not in the outer office but Gavin Black was there, searching through a filing cabinet.

"He's inside and he's alone," he beamed, nodding at the closed door to Dante's office.

She found him seated behind his desk, speaking on the phone. Acknowledging her arrival with nothing more than a faint lift of his eyebrows, he swiveled to face the window and continued his conversation.

It was a far cry from the welcome she'd envisioned. His mind's on other things and small wonder, Leila told herself. Hadn't she been swamped with work when she came back from her buying trip to the Orient?

Perching on one of the chairs flanking the other side of the desk, she tried to allay her growing sense of uneasiness by feasting her eyes on the sight of him.

He needed to visit the barber. Instead of lying flat and close against the nape of his neck, his hair curled a little. But the hand cradling the phone was exactly as she recalled, lean and strong and capable of awakening such passion in her that she grew weak at the memory of it.

Something the other party said annoyed him. Swinging around, he rapped a pencil on the desk. "Restrictions on the export of antiquities from the country of origin are becoming more stringent all the time," he snapped, "so don't tell me this is only a minor glitch. We're facing an increasingly diminishing supply for a growing demand and unless we want to lose clients, we need to find new markets."

His eyes were shadowed with fatigue, his mouth bracketed with lines of frustration. Unable to help herself, she leaned across the desk, intending to stroke back the hair from his forehead. But the way he abruptly swiveled away again, without once making eye contact with her, tightened her misgivings into a knot of anxiety lodged just beneath her breastbone.

Slipping out of the chair, she went to stand at the other window in his corner suite. Outside it was beautiful, one of those early west coast April mornings full of plum blossoms, tulips and promise of sultry summer days to come. The mountains reached snowy tips to the north. To the west, the waters of Georgia Strait reflected a sky of such primary blue that it might have been lifted straight from a child's paint box. Sandwiched between the two, the office towers of downtown Vancouver picked up the mirror image and flung it back as though to challenge nature with their own brilliance.

It was, quite simply, an exceptional setting in which to welcome home an exceptional man. A day which surely could only get better as she renewed acquaintance with her lover, and she was letting her imagination get the better of her by supposing otherwise.

From all accounts, pregnant women were at the mercy of their hormones and apt to be irrational at times. He was tired and distracted, that was all. Wasn't it?

The phone receiver clicked into place on its console almost as sharply as he rapped out, "You wished to see me?"

His tone was so cold that her first thought was that someone else had entered the room without her realizing it. But then she saw that there were still just the two of them and he was not approaching her or giving any indication that he was glad to see her.

Instead he remained behind his desk, leaning back with his hands resting on the arms of his chair and his expression, which moments before had reflected irritation with company concerns, now betrayed nothing but the stony indifference of a man annoyingly importuned by a stranger.

To the casual observer his behavior might have been passed off as the result of business woes or jet lag, but a lover's intuition was too finely attuned to be so easily reassured. Even without the corroboration of Carl Newbury's self-satisfied smirk minutes earlier, Leila knew that her first instincts had been correct.

Something was terribly wrong. Where before warmth and incorrigible passion had flared between her and

Dante, a frigid calm now ruled, turning the knot of trepidation still snagged near her heart into a certainty as hard and immovable as a stone.

"Of course I wish to see you, Dante," she said, dismay leaving her breathless. "I've missed you. The last four weeks have seemed interminable."

"You surprise me," he said. "I wouldn't have thought you'd find enough hours in the day to attend to your many...affairs."

Where other men might wound with words, he managed to sear with silence. That telling little pause before he said "affairs" imbued the term with such a wealth of contempt that she flinched.

Of course, she guessed at once what he meant. "When will you tell Dante?" her mother had asked that morning, referring to the situation with Anthony.

"The very first chance I get after his plane lands," she'd replied blithely. "There's no keeping it a secret even if I wanted to, and I'd hate him to learn about it from someone else."

But he'd arrived home hours ahead of time and she knew she had not, after all, been the one to break the news to him, just as surely as she knew who had. Still, she tried to bridge the chasm of his hostility by appealing to him with her hands held out and saying softly, "If you're referring to Anthony Fletcher— "

His brows shot up in mock surprise. *"If?"* he echoed scornfully. "You mean there are others besides him?"

"Don't do this, Dante," she begged, cut to the quick by his sarcasm and his absolute refusal to acknowledge her efforts at conciliation. "At least let me explain the situation before you judge me and find me guilty."

"What's to explain?" he shot back. "It was all spelled out in last week's paper, complete with very explicit pictures."

"I was hoping we'd have a chance to talk before you saw that."

"And I was willing to give you just such an opportunity. I waited here all day Friday, expecting you to show up. It seemed a reasonable enough assumption, given that you're being paid to put in a full week's work. But you chose not to make an appearance." His smiled coldly. "Or else you forgot. I guess anyone might when a lost fiancé suddenly resurfaces to remind a woman of where her future is likely to be best served."

"Wait a minute!" she cut in, caught off balance yet again. "You were here on Friday? I had no idea."

"Clearly not."

"Why didn't you call me at home?"

"I did, several times. There was no answer."

"No," she said, "Of course there wasn't. We—my mother and Cleo and I—"

Had gone to see the doctor: a straightforward excuse that could easily be verified, but not one she felt inclined to divulge just then. He was in no mood to learn she was expecting his baby. That magical recognition of two souls destined for one another, that spark of instant, irrefutable physical attraction which they'd known on Poinciana, appeared, at least for him, to have died as swiftly as they'd arisen. The way he was looking at her now, with such withering scorn that she wanted to crawl into a dark hole and hide, spelled utter disillusionment for everything she represented.

"We went out for lunch," she said lamely, deciding half a truth was better than none. "I had to explain to them—about Anthony."

"And *my* mother?" he blazed. "Did you bother to explain to her? Or did you think it was quite okay for her to draw her own conclusions when she found the whole sordid story splashed all over the front page of the local rag?"

Dots of perspiration beaded along her hairline at the realization that, in all the uproar of the last three days, she'd completely overlooked the impact the news would have had on Dante's family. The enormity of her over-sight was, she knew, inexcusable.

"Dante," she said, retreating before his justified wrath, "I'm so sorry! I didn't think—"

"Yes, you did," he said, almost exploding with rage. "Whatever else you didn't do, you thought! What I mistook for charming reticence was nothing more than a calculated coverup on your part."

He struck a pose and mimicked, "'Oh, Dante, let's be more discreet. Let's keep our affair secret.' Well, no wonder! I was just an amusing diversion, wasn't I? Something to keep you entertained until Mr. Right floated back on the scene. How convenient that we conducted our little romance on a private island miles away from here. Now that all the dots are connected, it makes for a far different picture from what I'd originally imagined."

"Stop it!" she cried. "You know that's not how it was!"

"Bull!" he sneered. "That's *exactly* how it was. And I guess the laugh's on me for being so readily taken in by a woman who apparently believes in keeping a stash of men in reserve in case the candidate of choice doesn't quite pan out as she hopes, but that doesn't prevent me from finding you despicable."

With each word he stalked her until she was pinned against the far wall like a butterfly. His anger scorched the air from the room and left her panting as if she'd run a mile uphill during a heat wave.

The nausea she'd thought was under control rose up with renewed vengeance.

"You couldn't be more wrong," she said weakly, plucking at the collar of her blouse in an attempt to fan a cooling draft over her skin. "Dante, you have to know you're the only man who has my love and loyalty. Anthony and I were involved for a time before I met you, but never the way the newspapers made it seem."

"Then I feel very sorry for Anthony. I know exactly how he must feel."

The room was growing darker around the edges and his voice was fading in and out in rhythm with the wavering shape of him. "No, you don't," she panted. "If you'd just let...me explain, you might...view him and me...in a more compassionate light."

From a very great distance, Dante said, "I doubt it, honey. I sincerely doubt anything you—"

His sudden silence, coupled with the penetrating stare of his eyes, so deeply aquamarine that she could feel herself disappearing into their depths, washed over her in blessed relief.

And then his voice began again, closer, touched with a different kind of edge. "What's the matter with you?"

She dared not answer. She was afraid that, if she opened her mouth, she'd be sick all over him. Only the darkness promised relief and all she wanted was to sink into the oblivion of its silent embrace.

He would not let her. Gripping her upper arms, he hauled her to one of the couches and forced her head down between her knees. "Meg, get in here," he shouted.

Leila heard the door open, and footsteps. Saw the thick, unlovely ankles of his assistant, whose sweetness of temperament more than made up for her physical imperfections. "Take a deep breath, Leila," she crooned, placing a cool hand on the nape of Leila's neck. "That's the way. Now another."

At length the shifting pattern of the rug beneath her feet grew still enough that Leila dared lift her head. Dante loomed on the periphery of her vision.

"Can't you see she's about ready to pass out, Dante?" Meg said sharply. "Don't just stand there, for heaven's sake! Bring a glass of water."

"No." Bracing both hands on the couch, Leila struggled to stand up. "I don't need anything."

It wasn't quite the truth. She needed Dante, but not like this. Not with his eyes full of suspicion and every line of his body rife with bitter resentment.

"You don't look too swift to me," Meg said. "What happened? Did you forget to eat breakfast?"

Leila shuddered. If only people wouldn't keep referring to food!

"Drink the damned water," Dante snapped, shoving a glass into her hand so abruptly that drops showered over her skirt.

"No wonder you decided to take the import world by storm," Meg informed him. "If this is your idea of a bedside manner, you'd have made a lousy doctor."

Scowling, Dante said, "Get back behind your desk, Meg. The crisis appears to have passed."

"Yes, sir, Mr. Boss!" She saluted and marched to the door where she stopped just long enough to add saucily, "Don't let him fool you, Leila. This is just his way of covering up the fact that he's scared spitless at the thought that his special lady might be ill. These strong, silent types are all the same—prepared to wrestle a tiger with their bare hands but useless in a minor crisis. He's probably afraid of the dentist, too."

Beyond a towering glare, Dante let the observation pass and waited until Meg had closed the door behind her before addressing Leila again. "If that little effort was a ploy to gain sympathy," he said, "I can tell you now that it didn't work."

She stared at him, too depleted in body and soul to muster the energy to defend herself against this latest attack. "I'm not that good an actress, Dante. And even if I were, I don't feel I have to resort to cheap deception to justify myself in your eyes. Believe what you will. It's clear you've already judged me and found me guilty."

He watched as she set the glass on his desk. Thanking providence and Miss Carstairs who'd been her governess and who'd believed that good posture, like cleanliness, was next to godliness, she held herself erect and walked out of his office. Not by so much as a blink did she betray the fact that her knees had turned to jelly and her legs felt weak as water.

But once in her own office she literally crumpled, shaken not just by the evaporation of all her dreams and hopes but by what now struck her as a lamentable lack of judgment and intelligence.

Her mistake had not been in allowing Dante to beguile her. Even in her present dire misery, she knew the odds were slim that she'd ever have found the strength to withstand his seduction. But how could she have known that what had struck her as the love of a lifetime just two short months ago could wither in the virtual blink of an eye? As easily as stepping on a bug, Dante had ended it and she had been foolish beyond words to allow him such free access to her heart.

And to her body. May God forgive her, she'd conceived a child by a man who despised her! Oh, if only she could turn back the clock…!

Covering her face with her hands, she rocked back and forth in her chair and let the tears she'd suppressed in front of him run free. She'd known sadness before. Her father's suicide, the poverty and loneliness to which her mother had been reduced, even Anthony's disablement: each had caused its share of grief and misery. But none compared to the gaping hole left by Dante's defection.

Eventually, though, the tears dried up. A person could cry for only so long before she realized that it didn't change anything. The original problem still remained and no amount of cataclysmic weeping eased the pain of a broken heart.

Somehow she had to drum up the strength to go on; to take control of her life again. Work was supposed to help, she'd heard, and heaven knew she had plenty to keep her occupied. Her shipment of samples had arrived and needed to be unpacked and set up in the main floor showroom.

So she worked all morning with an energy bordering on fever, stopping for nothing, not even lunch. The tea Gail brought her around one remained untouched on her desk. In the afternoon, she tackled the paperwork so that, by five when everyone else went home for the day, her files were up to date, all the messages from Friday returned, all the forms required by customs' brokers attended to.

If anyone had looked in her office, they'd have seen a woman apparently too engrossed in cataloging different qualities of Korean celadon pottery to realize the working day was over.

Only when the special silence of a building empty of all activity closed over her did she shut down her computer. Only when she was sure no one would witness the collapse of the facade she'd presented did she lean her head against the back of her chair, close her eyes and confront a future vastly different from the one she'd foreseen when she'd stepped out of bed that morning.

She was going to bring a baby into the world who would not know its father. Through her own wilful self-indulgence and blind carelessness, her son or daughter would be deprived of every child's birthright: a normal home with two loving parents.

Always assuming he recognized the baby as his, instead of sharing the joys and pleasures of parenting, she and Dante would divide them. There would be holidays spent apart from her child; birthdays and Christmases when her only contact might be through a phone call.

She had lived in Canada long enough to know that was how things were done when adult relationships came to an end, and she found the idea insupportable. Whatever her father's ultimate shortcomings, he had

never let her down when she was young as she would
be letting down her child.

"Oh, I could learn to hate you, Dante," she sighed
brokenly, choking back a fresh onslaught of tears.

"The feeling's mutual, I assure you."

His voice lanced her from across the room, unexpected and devastating in its impassioned certainty.
Startled, she shot bolt upright in the chair and found him
leaning in the doorway, watching her.

"What are you doing here?" she snuffled, groping for
the box of tissues in the top right-hand drawer of her
desk. "Everyone else has gone home."

"I could ask you the same thing," he said, shoving
himself away from the door frame and strolling into the
room with one hand jammed into the pocket of his gray
flannel slacks.

"Is this why you came looking for me, Dante?" she
said wearily. "So that we can go 'round in circles, tossing the same question back and forth between us and
getting nowhere? Haven't we done enough of that for
one day?"

"I'd say we've done plenty."

"Then what do you want?"

His jaw tightened almost imperceptibly. "Truthfully?
I don't know."

Against her better judgment, a spark of optimism
sprang alive inside her. Maybe it was the dejection in
his posture, or the pain darkening his eyes that made her
dare suggest, "Could it be that perhaps you're ready to
hear my explanation before you consign me—us—to the
garbage heap?"

He sighed then, the way a man might when he sees
that if he's ever to know peace of mind again, he's going
to have to swallow his pride and admit to the facts, no
matter how unpalatable he might find them. "Okay, I'm
listening," he said.

So she told him everything that had happened in the

last few days, leaving out nothing except the part about the baby. She would not, she vowed, barter her child to win his belief or forgiveness. On that point there would be neither negotiation nor compromise.

"I visited the Fletchers several times since Anthony came home," she finished, "and eventually straightened everything out."

"How did they take it?"

"It wasn't particularly easy or pleasant for any of us."

Pleasant? It had been an occasion only slightly less horrendous than Dante's even more volatile reaction! Gloria Fletcher had not taken kindly to the idea that anyone, particularly a woman whom she perceived to be of inferior social rank, should decline to have her name linked to the Fletchers.

As for Anthony...! Poor man, he had been utterly bewildered and devastated.

"But," she told Dante, "to tell them anything less than the absolute truth struck me as immoral and inhumane."

"All very plausible and praiseworthy, I'm sure," he said, "except for one thing. Fletcher's head injury might have addled his brains, but the last I heard, amnesia isn't contagious. So how come his parents had conveniently forgotten you and he were no longer an item?"

"Because he never told them otherwise. It could have been that he left the country the day after we broke up and had too many other things on his mind, or else..."

She hesitated, unsure how much to reveal of that last meeting with Anthony, the night before he flew to Croatia. He'd driven her up one of the local mountains and with the whole city spread out at their feet, he'd asked her to marry him as soon as he came home again.

"But I can give you everything!" he'd protested, stunned when she'd turned him down. "Money, prestige, entrance to the best social circles." He'd indicated the

millions of twinkling lights below them. "Marry me,
Leila, and all this will be yours."

He hadn't understood that it was what she couldn't
give him that mattered, namely her heart.

"Or else what?" Dante prompted.

She met his gaze and saw the skepticism lingering in
his eyes. "Because his pride wouldn't allow him to believe me when I told him I didn't want what he was
willing to offer," she said, "just as yours won't allow
you to believe me when I tell you that I love only you."

His glance slid away from hers at that and for a long
while he didn't say anything. He drummed his fingers
on the edge of her desk. Went to the window and stared
out. Cleared his throat and fiddled with the cord on the
blinds. And eventually—*finally*—swung back to face her
and with something approaching his old passion, said
ruefully, "The poor bastard. No wonder he took off for
Croatia. It must have seemed like heaven compared to
the hell of not being able to have you."

She didn't know who made the first move after that,
nor did she care. All that mattered was that they met
halfway around her desk and that he held her in his arms
as if he'd never let her go again. And stroked her face
as if she were the most precious creature ever born. And
murmured words of love and apology and self-
condemnation, mixing them all up with kisses full of
hunger and flavored with fire.

But it wasn't enough to ease the heartache or to erase
the doubts and misgivings so recently endured. She
needed more—tangible proof that her instincts when first
she'd met him had been right; confirmation that destiny
had always been on their side. She needed to recapture
what they'd come too close to losing.

Goaded by fear and wishing she was more skilled in
the art of physical loving, she clung to him, imprinting
herself inch for inch against him and praying that she
could incite him to the same raging hunger that con-

sumed her. Because wasn't it then, when a man and a woman shared the ultimate intimacy, that they opened their hearts to each other without reservation?

Or was it entrapment of the most ancient kind, a manipulation of feminine power over a man when he was at his most vulnerable?

No! Ignoring the voice of conscience, she tugged at Dante's shirt, freeing it from the waist of his slacks and opening it against his chest. With an aggression unlike any she'd shown before, she pressed her lips to the warm skin covering his heart. Flicked her tongue over his nipple.

His response was swift and unmistakable. The leap of his blood pulsing through his veins, the urgent thrust of his flesh, the ragged, painful rasp of his breath, spelled only one message. She had succeeded beyond her wildest expectations. He was on fire for her.

What chance had moral rectitude or self-preservation against such intoxication? Oblivious to the fact that the office cleaners could walk in at any moment and discover them, she lay half sprawled beneath him on the desk, while the papers she'd taken all afternoon to sort into neat and separate piles fluttered to the floor like so many flakes of snow flying before the wind.

Her only awareness was of her hands frantic at his fly, of her skirt riding up around her hips and his finger reaching inside her panties to torture her.

She could not endure the cruelty. Driven wild by the heat of his mouth at her throat, at her breast, she whimpered his name, only to lose the last syllable in an explosive sigh of release as he spun her around and, bracing himself on the edge of the desk, pulled her astride him and drove into her.

It was not a graceful coupling. It was desperate and frenzied and undignified. Much later, when it was too late to repair the damage she'd done, she would realize that what she'd initiated in those too brief seconds had less to do with love than with desperation, but at the time she did not want to admit to such a thought. At the time she thought that the shuddering of his powerful body and her own molten surrender were enough to erase the damage they'd inflicted on their relationship and a guarantee against future doubt and mistrust.

"I didn't come here intending for this to happen," he said, when it was over.

"Are you sorry it did?"

He pulled her clothing into place again with great tenderness. "I should be. There's more to making a relationship work than sex, yet when I'm around you I lose all perspective. You make me crazy, Leila. That's all the explanation I can offer for acting like such a boor this morning." A grimace of disgust touched his mouth. "I don't like to think of myself as a man given to violence but the thought of you with another man—"

"Please," she said, covering his mouth with her fingertips. "Let's not go over it all again."

"No," he said, taking a small velvet pouch from his pocket. "Let's not."

Thanks to her father, Leila knew a good deal about gems; enough, certainly, to recognize the superb quality of the diamond which Dante let slide into his hand. The clarity and cut of the stone were flawless, the elegant simplicity of its setting breathtaking.

"If you were wearing this," he said, slipping the ring on her finger, "everyone would know you belong to me."

An hour ago she had wept for all that she thought she had lost. Now sheer happiness brought her to the brink of tears again. Or had it all come about too quickly, too easily? Was this yet another example of wilful naïveté on her part?

"Now that I know Fletcher's out of your life," Dante said, seeing her hesitation, "there's no reason we can't make our engagement official, is there?"

The question brought back all the demons which had haunted her earlier. They were trying too hard to make things right again. It would take more than a Band-Aid solution like a diamond ring to restore what they'd once shared. "Anthony isn't out of my life, Dante," she said quietly.

"Why the hell not, if, as you claim, you've ended things with him?"

"I never said I'd 'ended things.' I said I'd cleared up the misunderstandings."

"Same thing," he snapped, his eyes shooting sparks of fire. "Stay away from him, that's all."

"No. He's my friend and right now he needs me."

Dante raked furious fingers through his hair. "He's the reason you and I are off track, for crying out loud!"

"No, he isn't," she said sadly. "You and I are the reason. And if you think my wearing your ring gives you the right to determine who my friends are, we'll be staying off track."

"Damn it, Leila, I won't tolerate this."

"Then go back to your import accounts and forget this," she said, taking off the ring and handing it back to him. "Because I don't want a control freak for a husband."

"And I don't want another man's leftovers!" he bellowed. "Carl was right. You're nothing but a cheap—"

As though realizing he'd gone too far, he pulled himself up short, but the damage was done. Newbury had been her declared enemy from the start, but that his poison had infected a man of Dante's stature devastated her.

Slowly, she stood up, though truth to tell she needed to lean against the side of her desk to counteract the dizziness that swept over her. "By allowing Carl Newbury to prejudice our relationship you have tainted every lovely thing we ever shared," she half whispered, "and I don't know if I'll ever forgive you for it."

He looked ashamed, but too proud to reverse things

before further rot set in. All it would have taken was an apology. Even at that late stage, if he could have bent enough to say, ''I'm sorry,'' she would have forgiven him.

But she saw the stubborn cast to his mouth, the proud arrogant bearing, the unveiled anger in his eyes. So what was the point in prolonging the agony? In the space of a few minutes, he'd destroyed the most glorious months of her life. He was not the man of her dreams, after all.

CHAPTER SIX

DANTE hunched over the table and stared moodily into his predinner Scotch. He was in no mood for entertaining the clients who'd blown into town that morning on a moment's notice from Buenos Aires.

From his seat opposite, Carl Newbury alternated between watching Dante and keeping an eye on the visitors, who'd gone out on the restaurant balcony with Rita and Gavin to admire the view.

At length he cleared his throat and said, "You seem preoccupied, boss. Down in the mouth, even."

Small wonder! He'd always thought having five sisters made him an expert on women but, somewhere along the way, he'd obviously missed a lesson because he clearly hadn't the foggiest idea what made the female mind tick. He couldn't see what was so unreasonable about a man expecting his fiancée to abandon an ex-boyfriend, but the way Leila had reacted, anyone would think he'd asked her to trade in her firstborn.

Of course, he never should have brought Carl into things. He'd never set any store by the man's opinions and knew the only reason he'd even mentioned his name had been a skewed attempt to give her back a dose of her own medicine.

"Dante? Anything wrong?" Carl never did know when to back off.

"I'm tired," he said, uncaring that he sounded short. "A lot piled up while I was away and I've got enough on my mind without having to wine and dine overseas clients before my suitcase is properly unpacked."

"Ah!" Newbury downed half his martini and pursed

his lips in what Dante could only suppose was an attempt to encourage some sort of male bonding. "Would one of those things be Leila Connors-Lee, by any chance?"

Three months ago, no one in the company would have dared ask such a question. That Newbury did now, without any attempt to disguise his bald-faced curiosity, both offended and infuriated Dante. "Where the hell do you get off asking me a question like that?" he snarled.

Newbury reared back and raised his hands in exaggerated surrender. "Hey, sorry if I was out of line. It's just that...well...."

The phoney reluctance didn't fool Dante for a minute. Carl was onto something and itching to share it. "Well, *what?* You might as well finish what you've started, Carl. You've said too much to stop now."

The other man raised his eyebrows and took his time fishing the olive out of his glass before replying. "There's talk that you and our Miss Connors-Lee have had a falling-out. The way I hear it, she left your office in tears yesterday morning and has been pretty much incommunicado ever since. Naturally I assumed that business with the Fletcher heir had been the last straw and you'd finally seen her for the pushy opportunist she is."

Dante resisted the urge to plant his fist in the middle of Newbury's self-satisfied face. He knew some of his colleagues thought he'd lost his marbles in the Caribbean and was making a damn fool of himself. And in all fairness, he couldn't deny that he'd given them cause.

Not normally a man given to reckless behavior, he'd indulged in one impulse after another from the moment Leila walked into his life and now he was paying the price. But he was damned if he'd sit meekly and let Newbury rub his nose in the fact. Which was the only explanation he could offer for what he said next.

"I'm afraid you've got it all wrong, pal. Leila and I are as tight as ever. In fact, we're all but engaged."

The lie was almost justified, if only to see the effect it had on Newbury. "Cripes," he bleated, and drained his glass. "When's the happy day?"

"Not for some time." Stunned that he'd allowed blind impulse to coerce him into yet another untenable position, Dante attempted to brush the subject aside.

Newbury, however, was not about to be sidetracked. "I've got to hand it to you, Dante. You've got guts. Jumping into marriage after everything that's happened…" He shook his head, the gesture conveying a mixture of pity and contempt. "In your place, I'd have washed my hands of her."

Dante was under no illusions about Carl's real feelings toward him. Unlike his vice president, who'd been born with the proverbial silver spoon in his mouth, and who'd added to his blue chip background by an advantageous marriage, Dante had reached the top the hard way, earning his way through college on scholarships and taking part-time work wherever he could pick it up.

During the winter and spring semesters, he'd delivered take-out pizza in the evenings and on weekends. Summers, he hired himself out to one of the logging camps, turning his hand to whatever job needed to be done as long as it helped pay the bills. Given the circumstances, he'd had little other choice.

What he didn't have was a pedigree as long as his arm. He'd never had the time or inclination to join a fraternity, and when his father's death had left his mother to raise five teenage daughters alone, he'd quit university and taken a job as a warehouse foreman, putting in eighteen-hour shifts, six days a week, to make sure the family had a roof over its head and bread on the table.

But he'd never given up on his dream to do better than his father and grandfather. Not for him a life of working to make another man rich. So when the opportunity arose to learn the import business from Gavin Black and rescue Classic Collections from the brink of bankruptcy, Dante recognized his chance and grabbed it. He'd worked his way up to where he was today. Partner and CEO. On top. In charge.

He'd secured that place by exercising integrity and judicious restraint, not by blowing off about something on which he couldn't guarantee delivery. So what did he think he was doing, announcing to Newbury of all people, that he and Leila were as good as engaged? In light of yesterday afternoon's fiasco of a reconciliation, a congenital idiot would have known better.

Burying a sigh, he forced himself to acknowledge another painful truth. What he lacked in fancy letters behind his name, he made up for in bullheaded determination and pride. He could put up with a lot from other people—nobody was perfect, after all—as long as they didn't take advantage of his family or try to make a fool of him. That he'd allowed Newbury to push him into making a fool of him*self* he found both inexcusable and intolerable.

But did he back off? Take a little time to regroup? Hell, no! Savvy, streetwise Dante Rossi blundered on, trying to cover his tracks and succeeding only in miring himself deeper in trouble.

"I guess that's the difference between us, Carl. I know a good thing when I see it," he said, staring Newbury in the eye and not backing down an inch.

"The question is, Dante, do you know enough?"

Your pride won't let you believe I love you, she'd said when they were duking it out over Fletcher, and in his heart he knew she was right. Was he going to keep making the same dumb mistake over and over until he really had lost her for good?

"If this is still about Leila, I know everything that matters."

"When you say 'everything,'" Newbury put in smoothly, "does that include the part to do with her father?"

You don't like to talk about your father, do you?

No.

Careful not to let it show that the question rocked his composure more than it should have, he said, "Her father's dead."

"I know. It's how he died—or more to the point, *why,* that concerns me."

"Well, it shouldn't," Dante said, signaling the waiter to bring another round of drinks. "You're not the one proposing to marry her, I am. And frankly, I find your curiosity more than a little odd. You take altogether too much interest in Leila's business, you know that?"

"Perhaps you don't take enough. I did a little background research on her that I think you'll find enlightening."

"I'd ask how you went about that, Carl, but I'm not sure I want to know."

"Oh, I didn't do anything illegal, if that's what's worrying you. But we've got contacts in the Orient that go back a long way. One phone call was all it took to get the goods on a man as prominent as the late Mr. Henry J. Lee of Singapore. He offed himself, Dante, and left behind a pile of debt which his estate didn't begin to cover and which his daughter is still scrambling to pay off." Newbury's laugh came insultingly close to a sneer. "The woman's agenda is clear enough. She's looking for someone to bankroll her, and if you ask me, you'd be a fool to hook up with her."

The contrary side of his nature had Dante wanting to see how far Newbury would dare to push him. The sane side decided to put an end to a subject which never should have been raised in the first place.

Leaning forward, he said in his deadliest tone, "But I'm not asking you, Carl. I never have, nor do I anticipate a time when I ever will. Frankly I find Leila's objectives regarding her father's debts admirable, so I'm not sure what it is you really have against her, apart from the fact that you think she robbed a buddy of yours of a promotion that was never coming his way to begin with. But I can promise you that if you continue this smear campaign against her, I won't let the fact that you're married to Gavin's favorite goddaughter stop me from booting you out of this company so fast you'll bounce. Do I make myself clear?''

Newbury's discomfiture was almost comical. ''You've misunderstood, Dante! My only concern is for you. I don't want to see you taken to the cleaners.''

''I can look after myself and you'd do well to remember that.'' Dante leaned back and smiled benignly. ''I see our visitors heading back our way. Smile, Carl, and try not to look as if you've just discovered a bee up your ass.''

He'd had the last word and left Newbury in no doubt about who was in charge. If only he could dismiss Leila as easily....

He'd have given his right arm not to give a hoot in hell about her or anyone connected with her. But the damnable truth was, despite the fact that they were poles apart in how they saw things, he still wanted her. And would do just about anything to keep her. Because the thought of any other man taking his place was enough to drive him over the edge.

She managed to avoid Dante for the next couple of days, in part because he was occupied with his Argentinian clients but mostly because she simply wasn't able to put in a full working week. Her nausea was just too severe, leaving her so drained that, by the Wednesday, she could barely drag herself home.

''You're losing too much weight,'' her mother said at

dinner that night. "Good heavens, Leila, except for around your middle, your clothes are hanging on you."

"Small wonder," Cleo said. "Look at her plate. She's hardly touched her food. When was the last time you ate a proper meal, sweet child?"

"I don't know," she said irritably. "Quite frankly, even if I weren't pregnant, the situation with Dante would be enough to kill my appetite."

Her mother tut-tutted with disapproval. "If you'd just tell him about the baby, I'm sure the two of you would work things out. You caught him at a bad time with the news about Anthony, dear. He's not normally an unreasonable man, I'm sure. He was charming to me."

Indeed he was, but there was another side to him, a mulish obstinacy her mother had not seen, and trying to explain it took more energy than Leila could spare just then. Affecting a nonchalance she didn't feel, she said, "I'm sure we'll work something out so stop worrying. As for my not eating...." She looked down at the piece of chicken on her plate. It looked back at her, glistening moistly next to its bed of peas and new potatoes. Trying not to gag, she pushed it aside. "Well, I guess it's all a normal part of being pregnant."

"No, it isn't," her mother replied very firmly. "The way you've been feeling—so dragged out and sick—isn't normal at all. I think you should see your doctor again."

In fact, Leila already had an appointment booked for early the following morning because, when she'd gone in the previous Friday, Margaret Dearborn, the obstetrician had had a cold. Not wanting to chance infecting her patient, she'd confirmed the pregnancy by using a test kit and had asked Leila to come back for a complete physical within the week.

"Hmm," she said, when Leila described her symptoms the next day, "I'm not sure I like the sound of all this. Hop up on the table and let's have a good look at you.''

The concentration with which she conducted the examination and the fact that she took so long over it did nothing to improve Leila's general sense of well-being. Recognizing the fine mist of perspiration that heralded another about of nausea, she took a deep breath and tried to relax.

Finally, the doctor stepped back and picked up her clipboard. ''It's too bad I wasn't able to check you out more thoroughly when you first came to see me,'' she said, scribbling furiously.

Not until that precise moment did Leila realize how badly she wanted Dante's baby. Nothing that had taken place between them since his return from Europe—not the disagreements, the disappointment or the heartache—could compete with the intense surge of protective maternal love she felt for the life growing within her. ''Something's wrong, isn't it? Tell me!'' she begged, more frightened than she ever remembered being.

Margaret stroked the bell of her stethoscope consideringly. ''For a woman only ten weeks into her first pregnancy, your uterus is considerably larger than it should be. Add this to your other symptoms, and it's my opinion that you're carrying twins.''

''Twins?'' Leila repeated as blankly as though the word had been plucked from a foreign language and meant nothing to her.

''Two babies,'' the doctor supplied, with a flash of humor no doubt brought on by Leila's stunned disbelief. ''But we won't know for certain until we do an ultrasound which I'll get my nurse to arrange for later on today.''

''I have to go to work right after I leave here. I've already missed too much time at the office.''

''My dear, if my diagnosis is on target—and I'm

ninety percent sure it is—missing time at the office is the least of your worries. The risk of premature delivery with twins is significantly higher than with single births and you're already operating under far too much stress. You're clearly exhausted and I can tell you now that if you seriously want this pregnancy to go to term, you're going to have to quit work.''

"But I can't!" She'd been depending on at least another six months' salary to pay off the last of her father's debts. "I need the money.''

"What about the father of these babies, Leila? Why isn't he coming forward and offering to help out with the financial end of things?''

"I'm sure he would," she said miserably, "if he knew I was pregnant.''

"You mean, you haven't told him?" The doctor looked shocked. "Why on earth not? Is he married to someone else?''

"No. We... I...just haven't found the right time—''

"When you yourself first found out was the right time, Leila, so what's really going on here? Are you afraid to tell him? Would you like me to talk to him?''

"No!" Good grief, the fallout from such an event didn't bear thinking about! If Dante had resented the way he'd learned about her relationship with Anthony, she couldn't begin to imagine his reaction at finding out from a third party that she was expecting his baby. Or babies!

"You see, that's just what I'm talking about," Margaret Dearborn said, slapping a blood pressure cuff around Leila's arm. "Believe me, either you follow my advice now or you'll wind up in a hospital bed before much longer. Unless, of course, you don't really want this pregnancy to last.''

"Well, of course I do!''

"Fine. Then tell the man before he figures it out for himself and enlist his support. Because you won't be

able to keep your condition a secret much longer and he
might take it amiss to discover he's the last to find out.
In the meantime, let's get you lined up for that ultrasound. Assuming it can be arranged for this afternoon,
I want you back here before the end of the day to discuss
the results.''

It had been the week from hell. The South Americans
had left at two that afternoon and he'd half thought he'd
ask Leila out to dinner and try to set things right between
them. But when he'd stopped by her office, he found
she'd called in sick that morning with some vague stomach ailment. He'd then phoned her at home, only to discover she was out.

"When did a four-day week become the norm around
here?'' he'd growled, slamming down the receiver.
"Sick, be damned! She's probably holding Fletcher's
hand again, if truth be known.''

Well, screw her! He'd wasted enough time chasing
her down. He couldn't find his desk for the work piled
up on it and he'd be a sight better employed tackling
that than spinning his wheels over her.

"Hold my calls, Meg,'' he barked into the intercom,
and waded into the mound of papers waiting for his attention.

He didn't lift his head again until Meg showed up at
his desk at the end of the day. "Anything else I can do
for you before I call it quits, Dante?''

Surprised, he saw it was past six already. "Heck, no,
Meg. Go home before your husband comes after me with
a shotgun. And take tomorrow off as a bonus for all the
extra hours you've put in this week. You must be
bushed.''

"You look rather drained yourself,'' she said, stack-
ing the letters she'd prepared for signing. "It's been a
pretty intense few days and I guess we're all feeling the
effects.''

"Yeah," he said, with more than a trace of sarcasm. "Either that, or there's something in the water around here. Apparently Leila didn't feel well enough to make it in to work today."

"I'm not surprised."

"Something to do with an upset stomach, I'm told."

"That's one way of putting it, I suppose."

Alerted by something in Meg's tone, he frowned. "You mean, you noticed she wasn't up to par?" he asked uneasily, wishing he hadn't been so quick to dismiss the idea that something might really be wrong with Leila.

"I could hardly help it. Apart from last Monday's episode here in your office, I've been in the ladies' room more than once this last week when she's made a dash for the nearest stall, and I recognize the signs all too well."

"No kidding! You mean you've got the same bug?"

"Lord, I hope not! Two's enough for me." Meg backed away from him as if he'd suddenly announced he had typhoid.

"Two what?" he mumbled, smothering a yawn.

"Children, Dante," she said. "What did you think I meant, puppies?"

The yawn evaporated, but his mouth remained gaping open. "Huh?"

"Offspring. Heirs apparent. Rug rats. You know, Dante—or you should. Your sisters have produced enough to form their own basketball team."

He must have looked every bit as dazed as he felt because she elaborated, "I'm talking about babies—of the human variety. The kind who grow into little ankle-biters and absorb every last cent you make with their unending need for new shoes, dental braces, summer camp and whatever the kid next door has that they don't."

"Are you trying to tell me that you think Leila is

pregnant?'' he said, at last finding his voice again. Except it didn't sound like his voice. It sounded like a badly rusted engine fallen out of some abandoned old car.

"Oh, jeez!" Meg turned an uncharacteristic shade of pink, a phenomenon which, all by itself, was enough to make Dante nervous. It took a great deal to rattle Megan Norris to the point that she actually blushed, and even more to make her babble as she then proceeded to do. "Hey, I shouldn't have opened my big mouth, Dante. I mean, I thought you knew…if—if there's anything *to* know, that is. I mean, everyone's aware the pair of you are an item, even if you aren't broadcasting it around the office. On the other hand, maybe she's just got the flu—there's a lot going around. Or something."

"Or something," he repeated slowly, and wondered how he'd managed to avoid seeing the obvious, because Meg was right. Over the last ten years or so, he'd witnessed a total of eleven pregnancies pretty much from start to finish and become such an expert on detecting the signs that, half the time, he'd figured out he was about to be made an uncle again before the mother-to-be had known for sure. So why hadn't he recognized what was wrong with Leila, for Pete's sake?

More to the point, why hadn't she come right out and told him herself?

Because it wasn't his baby?

"Dante?" Megan hovered at the corner of his desk, ready to bolt if need be. "Are you okay?"

"Sure," he said, pulling the stack of letters toward him.

It *had* to be his baby. If she was to be believed, she hadn't seen Fletcher in months until a week ago.

"Aren't you ready to pack it in for the day?"

If she was to be believed.

"As soon as I've signed these. But you go on home, Meg. You've done enough."

It *was* his baby! She'd been a virgin when they'd made love the first time. Which brought him back to full circle to the most crucial question: why hadn't she said something before now?

Granted, he'd been away for a month and last Monday morning might not have been the best time to spring the news on him, given the explosive atmosphere, but what about later that same afternoon, when they'd been so caught up with need and desire that they'd had leaped at each other all over her desk?

Or why not after that, when he'd offered her a ring? Why the hell would she have continued to keep quiet? She must *know*, for crying out loud! Even though this was her first, the symptoms were too classic to go unrecognized.

"If I spoke out of turn, Dante—" Meg said, refusing to get the hell out and leave him alone with his evil thoughts, "I really—"

"You didn't," he said shortly. "Good night, Megan."

He seldom addressed her so formally. She took the hint and scurried out of the office.

He waited until the door snicked quietly closed behind her before taking out a framed snapshot of Leila which he'd rammed into the top drawer of his desk almost a week ago. "So," he muttered, staring down at the perfect, guileless face, "you think you don't want my ring and you don't want me. Well, honey, if you're pregnant, you aren't going to have any choice. To paraphrase a line from a well-known movie, I'll make you an offer of marriage you can't refuse. Because no kid of mine is growing up a bastard."

Stuffing the picture back into the drawer, he reached for the phone and punched in her number again. This time, her mother answered on the third ring.

"I'm afraid she's not here," she said when he asked to speak to Leila.

"Really? I understood she was ill, but she's obviously feeling better."

"Er…yes." Poor woman, she sounded distinctly ill at ease. "I'm expecting her very soon, Dante. Would you like me to give her a message?"

"Yes," he said. "Tell her there's a small matter I'd like to discuss with her over dinner and I'll be by to pick her up in about an hour. And if you happen to speak to her again and she decides she has other errands to run before she comes home, please tell her not to worry about running late. I'll wait—all evening, if I have to."

CHAPTER SEVEN

DINNER with Dante? Out of the question!

"No, Mother," she said. "I just can't face him, not tonight."

"I don't think you have much choice, Leila. He sounded very determined. And you can't go on avoiding him forever."

"I can call and put him off."

"Save your energy, sweet one," Cleo advised, peering through the lace curtain at the parlor window. "He just pulled up at the gate."

Why was she surprised, Leila wondered. Her world had started spinning out of control weeks ago. The trouble was, she hadn't realized it until today when, suddenly, the simplest task had become too much for her. Her thoughts were scattered, incomplete, veering wildly from one problem to the next without resolving any.

How would she manage to pay off the last of the debts if she couldn't work? Where would she live? Cleo's house was barely big enough for three, let alone five. And most disturbing of all, how was she going to face Dante and tell him he'd fathered twins?

"Stall him," she said, firing the order at both her mother and Cleo. "I need some time to prepare myself for this."

It hadn't helped that the first person to accost her when she got home had been a man who, although he was a stranger, she had nonetheless recognized. Whether operating out of Singapore or Vancouver, debt collectors had a sameness about them that had less to do with specific physical features than general mien. The only difference lay in how she'd learned to deal with them.

"Go away," she'd said, brushing past the man on the path leading to the house. "I'm paying off my father's creditors as fast as possible, so please remove yourself from our property and don't bother us again."

He'd left. By law, he had to. But they'd send someone else, and sooner rather than later. They'd keep sending someone else, she thought gloomily, drying herself off after a quick shower and searching through her wardrobe for something comfortable to wear, until the last cent had been repaid. And in all truth, she had never wanted it any other way. Until this morning, it had not seemed so impossible a goal.

But her pregnancy had shifted everything to a new focus. She hadn't needed the late-afternoon appointment with Margaret Dearborn for confirmation of the morning's diagnosis. At the hospital, when the technician had pointed to the fuzzy images on the television screen, even Leila's untrained eye had been able to see two tiny hearts beating.

But none of that changed the fact that the happy-ever-after ending she'd so blithely envisaged with Dante had disappeared like mist in the heat of a summer sun. Their confrontation last Monday had done more than wound; it had exposed major flaws in the whole foundation of the relationship.

Oh, the passion still raged between him and her, insatiable and persistent even when things were at their worst. And she still loved him. Always would, she feared. She was indeed her mother's daughter in that respect: a one-man woman for life, no matter how rough the going might get, and she could not imagine ever experiencing with someone else the incredible meeting of body, mind and soul that she'd known with Dante.

But her belief that destiny was on their side, which had seemed so entirely plausible on Poinciana, no longer held firm. The intrusion of the real, all-too-imperfect world had displaced her fanciful notions of paradise.

"Leila," her mother called, tapping on her door, "Dante's growing impatient."

"I'll be right down," she said, hauling clothes out of her closet and discarding them, one by one. Hardly anything fit properly anymore. The only thing she could find that didn't make her look like a badly stuffed sausage was a straight-cut slubbed silk shift the color of ripe mangoes, and a matching jacket accented with satin lapels and buttons.

More glamorous than the occasion called for, the dress nevertheless slid over her hips without a wrinkle, the jacket camouflaged her thickening middle perfectly; they would have to do.

Looping a string of freshwater pearls around her neck and slipping on a pair of pale suede pumps, she drew a fortifying breath and braced herself to face the ordeal ahead. Because her mother was right: regardless of the sad state of affairs between her and Dante, she couldn't put off telling him the news any longer.

As if waiting to strike when she was too beleaguered to fight it, the nausea attacked again and sent her fleeing for the bathroom. She hated this part of being pregnant, she thought, repelled by the indignity of it all. The house was small, the bathroom located right near the top of the stairs, and Dante waited in the parlor immediately below. Could he hear her retching?

At length the spasm passed. Straightening up, she splashed cold water over her face. Doing so wreaked havoc with the little bit of makeup she'd applied, but how much did that matter when so many other, more urgent things clamored for attention?

He sat chatting affably enough with her mother and Cleo when Leila came down, but although he rose from the high-backed horsehair sofa at the sight of her and said, "You look very nice," she knew at once that his cordiality did not extend to her. His eyes were too coldly assessing, his smile too deliberate.

"I wasn't expecting to see you tonight," she said nervously, as soon as they were in the car. "What prompted you to ask me out?"

"I thought it was time we talked. We can hardly leave things the way they ended on Monday or pretend they never happened. We work in the same office, after all, and it's inevitable that we'll run into each other. It seemed a good idea to lay everything out in the open and arrive at some sort of mutually acceptable agreement on where we go from here."

"What do you mean by 'everything'?"

"I thought you might like to tell me," he replied shortly, his knuckles gleaming white around the steering wheel.

Her anxiety level rose another notch. She'd been right; he *was* full of anger and it was directed at her. "Are you upset about something—beyond the fact that we've had a falling-out, I mean?"

"Should I be?"

"No," she said, annoyance supplanting her dismay. "And if all you're going to do is answer a question with another question, we might as well abort the evening now because I don't have the energy for that kind of game."

He drove another few hundred yards along the main road before saying casually, "You don't seem to have energy for much of anything lately. You weren't in the office again today, I hear. Care to tell me why?"

Oh, no! Not with him in his present mood. She'd wait and hope a good meal would improve his disposition. "I had a couple of appointments elsewhere," she said and left it at that.

"I see," he said, and when it became clear she wasn't about to elaborate, switched to another topic. "And how is your good friend Mr. Fletcher? Or haven't you had time to see him with your busy schedule?''

"Interesting you should mention him," she replied, matching the irony in his tone. "As it happens, he's much improved. I spoke to him briefly yesterday and he told me his memory is gradually returning. Although he has no recollection of the days immediately prior to the accident, he does remember how things were left between us before he went away. He knows that we were never engaged and that I turned down his proposal.''

Dante braked for a red light and drummed a light tattoo on the steering wheel. "You're beginning to accumulate a lot of practice in that regard, aren't you?" he remarked. "First Fletcher, then me."

"I refused Anthony because I was never in love with him," she cried, stung that he seemed so wilfully determined to cast the worst possible light on her actions. "That was not the case with you."

"What was?"

"You and I have problems which, unless we find some way to resolve them, preclude our ever being happy together."

"What kind of problems, Leila? Be specific."

"Your lack of trust in me, for a start. I love you, Dante, but you seem more inclined to believe Carl Newbury's vicious gossip than anything I say or do."

He almost looked shamefaced. "Newbury's a jackass whose opinion doesn't mean squat to me. I was out of line even bringing up his name the other day, let alone implying anything his gutter of a mind could come up with might influence the way I see things."

"Well, that's nice to hear," she said softly, wishing he'd back the words with action. If only he'd reach for her hand, touch her arm, make some gesture, however small, in an attempt to bridge the estrangement between them.

But he appeared sunk in black thought, and with each second of silence, the distance grew wider, deeper.

When he did eventually speak again, what he had to say did nothing to mend matters. "Unfortunately, Leila, it doesn't alter the fact that you and I have arrived at an impasse. The bottom line is that we enjoyed a holiday romance which, by itself, is a harmless enough diversion. Our mistake lay in thinking we could predicate a marriage on it and I have to shoulder the greater proportion of blame for that. I've handled enough business deals to realize that no contract stands a chance of holding together unless it's based on cold logic and hard facts."

"What about emotions, Dante, or trust? Aren't they what a gentleman's agreement is all about?"

"They have no place in binding legal contracts. Emotions are too volatile, too ephemeral. As for trust, it's just a word and not worth the paper it's written on unless it's backed up by tangible proof it exists. I think you must agree we've already established that, you with your little secrets and me with my lack of faith."

The rain scurrying in from the Strait that afternoon had passed, leaving the sky to the west tinted with a soft melon sunset. The avenues were lined with trees drooping under the weight of damp pink blossoms. Lilacs were on the brink of bursting into bloom. The willow trees already had sprung their leaves. It was an evening for lovers, for strolling hand-in-hand along quiet streets and stealing kisses in the warm shadows.

But she and Dante, who only a week before had been so desperately, deeply in love that they'd thought nothing could ever come between them, sat like strangers, the rift between them impassable. She could have wept for the sadness of it all and had to bite her tongue to prevent herself from crying out, "Don't be so ready to give up on us! I need you to fight with me right now, not against me!"

But he wasn't the only one with pride and she'd have died before she let him see the extent to which he'd devastated her. "I daresay you're right," she said, striving to retain her composure. "But deciding to write our affair off as a business deal gone sour and behaving as if it never took place won't work, Dante, because I'm afraid it doesn't end there."

He swung into the restaurant parking and brought the car to a stop. "Really? Why not?"

"There's something you don't know. Something I should have told you about before now."

Stepping out of the car, he tossed the keys to the parking valet before coming around to hold open her door. "Am I going to like what I'm about to hear, or should I fortify myself with a good stiff drink before you unburden yourself?"

"I'm bowled over by your sensitivity," she said, unable to repress a flare of resentment. "Anyone would think I'm the one who suggested getting together this evening. If you find my company so intolerable, why did you bother bringing me here? I'm in no mood to enjoy soft music and candlelight and nor are you."

"You're right. But we're here now, and if it's all the same to you, I'd just as soon stay and order a meal. It's been hours since I last ate."

"You might find what I have to tell you kills your appetite. It's certainly taken the edge off mine."

Grasping her by the arm, he propelled her up the steps and into the restaurant. "Then I'll definitely order that drink first."

Once they were seated at their table, he immersed himself in the menu, looking up only long enough to inquire, "Would you care for a cocktail or shall I just order a bottle of wine?"

She'd never developed a taste for cocktails. Even when she'd attended her parents' glamorous parties where predinner drinks were *de rigueur,* the most she'd

take was a small sherry or dry vermouth. But at that
moment, with her courage and hope withering under
Dante's dispassionate stare, she could have downed a
double Scotch without blinking and come back for seconds.

It was just as well she was pregnant and alcohol was
off limits. "Neither, thank you," she said. "I'd prefer
sparkling water with a twist of lime."

He nodded at the waiter hovering at his elbow. "A
Perrier for my associate and a Scotch with ice for me."

Despite everything that had gone before, his use of
the word "associate" cut her to the quick. "How did
we end up like this, Dante? How could we have mis-
calculated so badly that we've gone from lovers to associates in less than a week?"

"Well, we're agreed that you're no longer my blushing bride-to-be, it doesn't strike me as tasteful to call
you my sex partner, and I'm a bit past the age where I
refer to women as girlfriends, particularly once the relationship has died, so what would you like me to call
you?"

"I don't know," she said miserably. "I only know
that you're not making it easy for me to say what I've
got to tell you."

"If you're waiting for me to beg you to confide in
me, honey, you're wasting your time. I've already been
on my knees to you once this week and I can't say I
relish the idea of doing it again. So either spit out whatever it is that's rattling you, or save it. It's up to you."

"Oh, I'll tell you," she said, hating the way he called
her honey, as if she were some cheap pickup he'd met
in a bar.

"I'm listening," he said.

She took a sip of water to steady herself. "First," she
said, "I'm leaving Classic Collections. I'll be handing
in my notice on Monday morning."

"The earth didn't move for me, Leila. If that's your

big news, rest assured we'll find someone else to take your place. Of more interest to me is why you've decided to quit.''

She stared down at her fingers, tightly linked in her lap. ''Because I'm pregnant, Dante.''

Well, hallelujah, she'd finally managed to spit it out! He'd begun to think he was going to have to drag it out of her a syllable at a time. ''Yes,'' he said calmly. ''I know.''

That shook her, as he'd known it would! She reared up in her chair as if she'd been electrocuted. ''You *know?*'' she gasped. ''That's impossible! I haven't told a soul except...oh, did my mother—?''

''I'm not a complete fool, Leila. I figured it out for myself, with a little help on the side from Megan Norris.'' No need to tell her Meg had practically had to draw pictures!

She glared at him, up to her pretty little earlobes in injured innocence. ''Then why didn't you say something before now?''

''Because I wanted to see how long it would take you to get around to telling me. And I think I finally figured it out.''

''There's nothing to figure out, Dante,'' she said, the flush which had briefly colored her face fading and leaving her pale with shock. ''Unless you're implying that the baby isn't yours.''

''Oh, it's mine, all right—I know a virgin when she's lying under me—but I think you wish it weren't. I think you'd far rather it were Anthony Fletcher's.''

''That's absurd!'' she exclaimed, and for a moment he almost believed her. Until she added, ''For a start, Anthony's no longer interested in me. He met someone in Croatia, an English nurse working with the Red Cross. As soon as he can arrange it, he's going back to look for her.''

"Jeez," he said, disillusionment almost choking him. "How bloody inconvenient and inconsiderate of him! Just when you needed him most, he ups and finds another love."

Just briefly, he wondered if he'd gone too far. She turned ashen and he was afraid she was going to pass out on him again. Against his will and certainly his better judgment, he almost reached out to touch her and tell her not to worry, that he'd take care of her.

But she had more stamina than a racehorse, despite her dainty frame and big, innocent eyes. Snatching up her bag, she pushed away from the table and said, "I have clearly deluded myself into believing that you're capable of caring about anything beyond your overweening pride and your unfounded jealousy of Anthony. Thank you for inviting me to dinner but I really don't have the stomach for it. Don't bother to drive me home. I'll call a taxi."

"Sit down!" he said, without a pang of regret at the tone he used, which he knew from experience could reduce obdurate clients to quivering surrender.

But she didn't so much as blink. She turned her back on him, her spine as straight and rigid as if she had a yardstick shoved up the inside of her dress, and marched away.

Almost blind with anger, he got up and raced after her, catching up with her just in time to see her disappear through a door near the entrance to the restaurant. Smacking it open, he followed her. "Don't you walk away from me!" he bellowed. "Whether you like the idea or not, that's my child you're carrying and I'm not about to be sidelined because I don't quite measure up to your standards of gallantry."

"Get out of here!" she hissed back. "You're in the ladies' room."

Oh, hell, he was! A quick glance at the little benches set before mirrors and the bowl of fresh flowers arranged on the vanity told him that. Men's rooms were a lot more basic, in design and function. But he was damned if he was going to let that deter him. "I don't give a flying f...fig!"

A toilet flushed behind the last of a row of smaller doors in an adjoining area and a woman with freshly permed hair framing her horsy face stepped into view. "Perhaps," she said, regarding him as if she'd seen better specimens lining the gutters of skid row, "she's right to expect more. I don't know which charm school you attended, young man, but I pray it's no longer in business."

"Speaking of business, madam," he snapped, trading glare for glare, "why don't you mind yours?"

Leila uttered a barely audible moan and rushed into one of the cubicles. Ignoring the outraged gasps of the society matron, he followed her in there, too.

She was bent over the bowl, her entire body heaving. Deftly, he supported her with an arm around her shoulders and waited for the retching to stop. At last she said weakly, "Please go away. I don't want you to see me like this."

"You think you're the first woman I've seen lose her lunch?" he said, leading her to the row of sinks and filling a paper cup with water. "I've got five sisters, remember? And they all put on the same floor show when they were pregnant. Here, rinse out your mouth."

"You might want to do the same with yours while you're at it," New Perm said tartly, apparently too fascinated by the drama taking place in the can to care that her lamb chops were growing cold at the table. "Your language is a disgrace. I'm going to call the manager and have you thrown out of here."

"I'll save you the trouble," he said, half carrying Leila toward the door.

"Please just take me home," she said, when he'd finally shoveled her limp body into the car.

"No," he said. "First, you need to eat, and second, we've got unfinished business to take care of."

"I can't eat," she said. "The thought of all that food is enough—"

"Then you can drink," he said, and took her to a place he knew from his university days where they made the best milk shakes this side of heaven.

"The lady will have vanilla, and make mine choco-late," he told the waitress, when they were settled in a booth conveniently close to the washrooms.

Leila said nothing until they'd been served, except to remark, "You don't strike me as the milk shake type."

"I guess that brings us back full circle to what you were saying earlier," he said. "We really don't know each other nearly as well as we thought we did, do we? Why, for instance, did you wait until tonight to tell me you're pregnant, Leila? Why didn't you say something on Monday when you practically passed out at my feet?"

"Because I didn't want to premise our relationship on the fact that I'm expecting your baby. I still don't want that. But I realize that you have a moral right to know about the pregnancy."

"Pity you didn't arrive at that conclusion before half the office was in on the secret."

She sighed and leaned her head on her hand. "I hadn't realized it was so obvious, though I suppose, in retro-spect, I should have. I'm falling so far behind in my work and leaving others to pick up the slack that it's no wonder the word's leaked out."

"And now that it has," he said carefully, "where do I fit into the picture?"

She pushed aside her milk shake as if it had turned suddenly sour on her. "Well I don't expect you to marry me, if that's what you're thinking. You've already dis-missed your feelings for me as nothing but a bad attack of tropical fever, and I—"

Her eyes filled with tears and he wished to hell she'd look somewhere other than at him. Those eyes, that face, made it very difficult for a man to keep his head. "You what?" he said brusquely.

"I can't trust my own judgment, let alone yours, because I'm afraid of the future," she said, completely falling apart. "It would be very easy for me to say I've changed my mind, and that I want us to go ahead with our wedding plans. But I know I'd be making that choice for all the wrong reasons."

He should have felt encouraged, elated even. At least she wasn't trying to con him. Instead he felt unutterably depressed. "So what do you want, Leila?"

She hesitated, seeming to roll her answer around inside her mouth as if not sure whether to swallow it or spit it out. Deciding in favor of the latter, even though it practically choked her, she said, "I need a loan. If you could see your way clear...I hate to ask, it sounds so mercenary...but I have to stop working because...."

By then, the tears were splashing down her face and onto the fake marble tabletop. "Go on," he said.

"Because I'm expecting twins and there's a risk I might miscarry if I don't," she wailed.

At that, he thought he might lose his own milk shake. "Huh?" he said.

"I'm having twins," she said again.

Struggling to contain his shock, he said, "And all you want from me is money?"

"It would just be a loan," she said again. "I'll repay it, as soon as the babies are born and old enough to be left. My mother and Cleo will look after them then, and I'll find a job. I wouldn't ask you, Dante, but I don't know who else to turn to. I don't have the collateral the banks require, and—"

They'd hit some rough spots in the last week. His pride tended to blind him to reason sometimes and he'd probably been somewhat hard in the way he'd handled matters. But as the evening progressed and despite himself, the suspicions he'd entertained about her that afternoon had begun to melt in the face of her distress.

She'd looked so frail and, even at her worst, still so beautiful, that he'd begun to believe they might be able to go back to the way things were, after all. Until she made it clear that she saw him only as a lending institution.

"I'll advance you the money," he said tightly, struggling to contain his anger.

Either she didn't notice his resentment or she didn't care. Her voice was breathless with relief when she said, "Thank you, Dante. I know what the going interest rate is at the major banks and I'll be happy to—"

"On my terms, Leila, not the bank's and most certainly not yours. I will assume full financial responsibility for our children and clean up the mess your father left behind. And in return—"

But he'd caught her off guard again. "What do you know about my father?" she whispered, her eyes huge with shock.

"Enough to be glad that I'm nothing like him. You're familiar, I'm sure, with the saying 'When the going gets tough, the tough get going'? Well, I'm one tough customer, honey. I've yet to back away from a fight and the moon will turn to green cheese before I put a gun to my head and leave a woman clean up the mess I leave behind. So, to continue with the terms of our contract, I'll take care of finances and you'll become the perfect corporate wife. In short, Leila, we'll be getting married within the month and no one needs to know that neither of us is wild about the idea."

"I can't do that!" she protested. "I *won't*. Women don't coerce a man into marriage these days because there's a baby on the way."

"And Rossi men don't let their children be born bastards, nor do they leave them to be farmed out while their mothers scrub floors to keep them in diapers.''

She cringed and pressed her palms to her belly, as if to shield the lives she carried from the savage brute confronting her. ''No!''

''I don't understand your reluctance, my dear,'' he said bitterly. ''You claim you still have some feelings for me. You're expecting my children. You need my help. And all I'm demanding by way of collateral on my investment is that you become Mrs. Dante Rossi. What's so difficult about that?''

CHAPTER EIGHT

SHE couldn't think of a reason in the world to refuse him. Everything he said was true. But sensible though all the other reasons were, the one that mattered most was that she loved him. Unreasonably, perhaps, given his brutal assessment of their relationship, and certainly irrationally. But when had logic ever entered the picture where he was concerned?

The bottom line was that she wanted him and she needed him. She was tired of swimming against the tide; tired of carrying her own and other people's burdens alone.

And if he didn't return her feelings in equal measure? Could she live with a husband who saw her only as a financial venture and the mother of his children?

She looked up and found him staring at her, his eyes the cool inscrutable aquamarine of a hard-driving businessman pressing to close a deal and not about to give an inch in the process. Yet the magnetism which had drawn her to him at their first meeting and which had continued to rage despite their efforts to conquer it, charged the atmosphere now, palpable as the crackling electricity before a summer storm and just as inescapable.

Given all that, didn't it make sense for her to agree to his terms? Wasn't it best for the babies to have a home with both parents? And if, meanwhile, she could love enough for both of them, might he not, in time, find himself falling in love with her again, this time for keeps?

Quickly, before conscience or reason could countermand the yearning conviction in her heart, she said, "All right, Dante, we'll do things your way. We'll be married."

She forced herself to match his tone, making her response sound flatly contractual, as if such calculated matrimonial agreements were the norm. She had to; it was the only way she could cope with the fact that, unlike his first impassioned proposal, this one amounted to nothing more than a corporate merger.

He continued to pin her in that cool, unfathomable gaze and let the seconds spin out between them in agonizing, judgmental silence. When she thought she could bear it no longer, he said with a contempt made all the more potent by his gentle tone, "So, you are to be had, if the price is right."

The accusation broke her heart, mostly because, from his viewpoint, it was justified. They'd lost so much—the spontaneity, the joy—and it was her fault. She had not intentionally deceived him when he'd asked her, in those early days, if there was another man in her life, but she had not been fully honest, either. Meeting Dante and falling headlong in love with him had consumed her to the extent that nothing she had known before—not Anthony, not her father's suicide and not her mother's straitened circumstances—had seemed relevant.

But even an innocent past caught up with a person sooner or later, as she was learning to her cost, and facts withheld took on a darkness they might not have assumed had they been revealed voluntarily at the outset, before emotions complicated matters.

Without ever intending to, she and not he had destroyed the trust they'd tentatively begun to establish. But if the fault was hers, so was the remedy. She would grasp at what was left of her relationship with Dante and cling to it in whatever way presented itself. Because for all that it bore the scars of their disenchantment, it was too precious and too rare to abandon; and because, if she did not hold it fast, it, too, would slip away and they'd never find their way back to each other.

"I'm not doing it for the money, Dante," she said. "I'm doing it for us because, despite everything, I still think we can make our marriage work if we try hard enough."

"You'll have a hard time persuading me of that, honey," he said, "but you'd better make damn sure you convince everyone else. Because understand this: you've made a fool of me for the last time and I will not have people sniggering behind my back, or pitying me for being the one left to clean up the mess when the other guy walked away."

His words shot arrows in her heart. *Remember why you're fighting to keep this man with you,* she told herself. *Remember not only that you love him but that, deep down, you believe he still loves you.*

She did not anticipate adhering to those beliefs would take such a toll. Could not, in her wildest imaginings, have foreseen the nightmare of what followed.

It started as early as the next morning. She was in her office, clearing out her desk, when her door burst open and Gail rushed into the room.

"Leila!" she exclaimed. "I'm so thrilled for you!"

Leila blinked, taken aback. "Why?"

"Oh, you can stop pretending—not that it was much of a secret to begin with, mind you!—but it's official now and I wanted to be the first to wish you well. Dante's a real hunk and could have taken his pick of any one of a hundred women, but he was smart and chose you. It's nice to know there's a heart as well as a brain under all those good looks."

"I gather," Leila said faintly, when the spate of compliments finally ran dry, "that you've heard about our…?"

"That you and Dante are engaged. Yes! Everyone read about it this morning." Gail stopped suddenly and clapped an exaggeratedly astonished hand to her mouth at Leila's blank amazement. "Except you, it seems! Good grief, you haven't checked the interoffice e-mail this morning, have you?"

"No," Leila said, refusing to believe Dante would choose such a coldly impersonal way to announce the news.

But he had. When she called up the morning's postings, there it was on her computer screen, sandwiched between a memo for all senior sales personnel to submit their latest client lists and a reminder that cars not showing a current company permit on the windshield were liable to be towed from the parking lot at the owner's expense: *I'm pleased to announce that Leila Connors-Lee and I are shortly to be married. Dante Rossi.*

Leila stared at the monitor, stunned. If his intention had been to belittle their engagement, he'd succeeded. While she was under orders to convince the world theirs was the love match of the century, he had no compunction at all about reducing it to the level of trivia.

"You don't look exactly radiant," Gail said, inspecting her sympathetically. "Still feeling under the weather, are you?"

"Yes," Leila said. "And let's not pretend we don't both know it's because I'm pregnant, Gail. Every other facet of my private life appears to be public domain, after all."

Gail looked uncomfortable. "It's no one's business but yours, Leila. I'm sorry if I've been intrusive."

"You haven't." Remorse flooded her. Friends had been hard to come by since she'd left Singapore, but Gail had been her ally from the day she'd started working at Classic Collections and deserved better than this. "I'm sorry. I'm being hypersensitive—a normal thing for expectant mothers, my doctor tells me, along with a lot of other unpleasant side effects, but that doesn't excuse taking out my frustrations on you."

"Hey, what else are friends for?" Gail squeezed her arm supportively. "In any case, you're the best thing that's ever happened in this department. Having a woman take over a senior overseas buyer's position and make such a smashing success her first time out has done wonders for female morale around here!"

"Thanks." From somewhere, Leila drummed up a smile. "I'm glad I'm good for something."

"You're terrific and Dante obviously thinks so, too. I've worked here nearly four years and in that time I've seen a fair number of women who've been smitten by that smile of his, and those incredible eyes. But it never registered with him. He was always the ultimate professional, Mr. Business down to his socks! The most personal thing he ever did was include a turkey voucher with the Christmas bonus cheques—oh, yes, and flowers for the office staff during Secretary's Week. Then you came on the scene and wham! You felled him with a single shot!" She sighed happily. "Gee, getting through the rest of the day's going to be tough after this, but I hear the phones ringing off the hook out there so I guess I'd better get back to my desk. Buzz if you need anything, Leila. Milk, antacids to calm an upset stomach, whatever, I've got them all!"

Oh, she needed something, all right, but it wasn't to be had out of a bottle! Last night it had been Dante's turn to lay down his terms, but today was hers. If he thought that her cultural background had predisposed her to being any man's doormat, he was about to find out differently.

"Had we scheduled a meeting?" he asked, when she marched unannounced into his office a few minutes later.

"No, Dante," she said. "I don't expect to have to make an appointment to see the man I'm about to marry, any more than I expect to find he's broadcast word of our engagement to the entire office without first consulting me on the matter. Or didn't it strike you as relevant that I might not want our private life made public?''

''I certainly had no idea you wanted it kept secret,'' he said, supremely unmoved by her obvious annoyance, ''although perhaps I should have, considering how reluctant you've been in sharing other aspects of your life with me.''

''I don't care if the whole world knows we're planning to be married,'' she retorted. ''It's the way you went about it that bothers me.''

''Really?'' He tapped the end of his pen on the surface of his desk. ''What, specifically, has you in such an uproar? It was brief and to the point but in no way insulting to you.''

''Neither would a typed sympathy note be to a person recently bereaved,'' she shot back, ''but it would show a marked lack of sensitivity on behalf of the sender.''

''You wanted me to hire a skywriter and advertise the event to the whole city, instead?'' he said scornfully. ''Sorry, Leila, but our supposedly red-hot love affair isn't front-page news around here any longer and most people, I suspect, wouldn't give a damn if we decided to exchange vows during a bungee jump. However, I am CEO of this company, as well as an equal partner, and common courtesy demands that my colleagues be informed. That being the case, I chose the most efficient way to tell them.''

''But not the most romantic.''

''What's romantic about a marriage based on money and desperation?'' He shrugged. ''Face it, Leila. You'd never have come to me for help if you could have found it elsewhere. You didn't even have the decency to tell me you're pregnant until I had you cornered. I heard it first from an employee, for crying out loud. Come to think about it, just about everything I've ever learned about the real you has come from someone else. A lot of men would take that as a very bad sign in a future wife and hedge their bets with an iron-clad prenuptial agreement.''

''If you feel like that, why are you so insistent on marriage at all? Why saddle yourself with a woman whom you clearly regard with the utmost suspicion?''

''You've just answered your own question, honey. I'm protecting my investment.''

''You don't need to marry me to do that,'' she said. ''I meant what I said last night. I'll sign whatever contract you draw up promising I'll pay you back every cent I borrow, with interest.''

''I'm not talking about dollars or cents, woman!'' he snapped, planting both hands flat on the desk and glaring at her. ''I'm talking about my children. You're a Singapore citizen, you travel on a foreign passport, and the only thing holding you here is your seventy-something mother and the debts she's saddled with. Do you seriously think I'm too stupid to figure out what could happen, once the creditors are paid off? You could leave this country tomorrow, before you give birth, and there'd not be a bloody thing I could do to stop you.''

''I would never do a thing like that,'' she gasped. ''Quite apart from the fact that my home is now in this country, our children are one of the chief reasons I agreed to the marriage in the first place.''

''It's your other reasons that bother me, Leila, and I'm not about to let them take precedence over the well-being of my children. If, for instance, you were lying last night and your feelings for me aren't all you cracked them up to be——''

''I wasn't lying,'' she said.

''Then we're both getting what we want out of this marriage. Agreed?''

She pressed her lips together. He was so much the proud lion, determined to hide his scars. She could only pray that her loving would heal them enough for him to relax his guard and let himself trust her again. "Agreed," she said.

"Fine." He nodded and handed her a sheet of paper. "In that case, you might want to look through this list of items needing attention if we're to pull a wedding together in the next couple of weeks. Feel free to add to it as you see fit. I'll leave the details to you and your mother, though if you choose to include my family, I know they'll be more than pleased to help. You'll see that I've made a note of our local church in case you don't know of one in your own neighborhood."

"You surprise me," she said, scanning the page. "I'd have thought, in view of the circumstances, that you'd have preferred a civil ceremony."

"Consider it a concession to your finer feelings," he said dryly. "Don't most brides want all the traditional trappings on their wedding day?"

"I'm not most brides, Dante. I don't plan to drift down the aisle in a cloud of tulle, white satin and misty-eyed wonder. That would be ludicrous, given the fact that I'm three months pregnant."

"As you wish." He shrugged again and reaching into the top drawer of his desk, tossed the velvet pouch containing the diamond ring across the desk at her. "Still, I want you wearing this, at least in public. It adds credibility to our arrangement, not to mention one of those visibly romantic touches you seem to think are important."

She made no attempt to catch the thing. It rolled across the desk and landed on the carpet with a soft thud.

Her small gesture of defiance brought the light of battle into his eyes again. "Pick the damned ring up and put it on your finger! It won't defile your dainty little hand. It's two and a half carats of the real thing, set in platinum and gold, not a chunk of glass and brass."

"It might as well be," she said, choking back the

tears. "Everything else about our relationship's a sham."

"Not quite everything, Leila." He came around the desk to retrieve the ring himself, then slid it onto her finger, and for one dizzying moment she thought she glimpsed a softening in his expression. When he laid a gentle hand against her stomach, her heart soared at the remembered sweetness of past embraces.

But then he said, "The children you're carrying are real enough. More to the point, they're mine and I don't intend ever to let you forget that, so let the ring act as a reminder."

"Will there be anything else?" she asked, afraid she couldn't hold back the tears much longer and wanting to be as far away from him as possible before they escaped.

"Just a couple. I explained to my mother all about your involvement with Fletcher and assured her anything she read in the papers was misleading. I also told her we'd brought the wedding forward and why."

"She knows I'm pregnant?" Instinctively, Leila placed her own hands where one of his had rested seconds before, as if doing so would conceal what was patently obvious.

"My mother's nobody's fool, Leila, even if she was bowled over by your apparent guilelessness when she first met you. She's had six children of her own and would have figured it out for herself eventually, I can assure you, but I wasn't taking any chances. I might have been the last one *you* chose to confide in, but I wasn't about to insult my family with the same shoddy treatment. So, yes, she knows and by now I'm sure my sisters do, too."

"And did your burst of honesty extend so far as to tell them that our marriage—?"

"No," he said, cutting her off with a slashing motion of his hand. "*That* is not their business, nor anyone else's, either. I meant what I said last night, Leila." He closed his fingers into a fist and held it in front of her face. "As far as the rest of the world goes, we're as tight as this! And you will do nothing to give anyone reason to think differently."

"I see." And she did, only too plainly. His pride was on the line and he was too busy protecting it to care that hers was taking a beating. "Anything else?"

"Yes. I've booked a private room at the Waterfront Hotel for this evening—nothing fancy, just a quiet family dinner to celebrate. I imagine you'd like to alert your mother to the fact, and Cleo, too, if you think she'd like to be included. Also, we need to find a place to live. If you feel up to it, I'll have an agent show you some houses next week."

"You don't want to stay in your penthouse?"

"It's not big enough. It has only one bedroom."

One bedroom had been enough before, she mourned, and the bed more than big enough for two. There hadn't been a place on earth too small for him to hold her and make love to her. A clearing by a mountain stream, a patch of moonlit sand, the turquoise, sun-hot waters of the Caribbean—how had those memories slipped away from him?

"I'd prefer something in the Shaughnessy area or the West Side," he went on, oblivious to her pain. "Commuter traffic's bad enough without fighting it all the way in from the suburbs. Also, I travel a lot and I'd like to be handy to the airport."

"Don't you want to be involved in choosing a new home with me?"

"I don't have the time. Make a short list of places you like and I'll check them out later. You shouldn't have any trouble finding something. Price is no great objective and there's a glut of high-end houses on the market these days. Oh, and one more thing. I've looked at my calendar and although I've got a heavy schedule for the next two weeks, I can take a couple of days off after that. So, I suggest we set Saturday the twenty-ninth as the wedding date.''

''Anything else?'' she asked faintly. He'd accounted for everything except the thing that mattered most: his loving commitment to their union.

''Not at the moment,'' he said. ''Unless something comes up in the meantime, I'll see you this evening.''

But something else did come up. The women in the office organized a little get-together in the boardroom to celebrate the engagement. Nothing too elaborate, just a few balloons and streamers, and a case of champagne courtesy of Gavin.

Leila had no inkling until she walked through the door, ostensibly for a hastily called meeting, and found herself confronting a party waiting to happen. Even Carl Newbury was there, his smile knowing.

''It's not good form to congratulate the bride, I know,'' he said snidely, ''but I think it's appropriate in this case. You're a very clever operator, Leila.''

Her nausea this time, she thought, sidestepping his attempt to engage her in further verbal sparring, had nothing to do with her pregnancy.

Dante showed up shortly after that and if he shared her dismay at finding himself center stage in a romantic farce, he did a much better job of hiding it. He played the lead without a single misstep, slipping his arm around her waist, beaming at the well-wishers and, when Gavin proposed the first toast, kissing her full on the lips with every appearance of ardor and enjoyment.

That he stared emptily into her eyes throughout and his mouth was hard as stone were but two more secrets to which only she was privy. No one else suspected, no one else questioned. She and Dante were, to all intents and purposes, the ideal couple, the bride appropriately shy and blushing and the groom masterful beyond compare.

"When's the happy day?" someone asked.

"A bit sooner than we'd originally intended," Dante said, proudly patting her stomach. "Leila's pregnant and we're both delighted, aren't we, sweetheart?"

"Delighted," she echoed faintly, near dying inside with embarrassment.

If playing a role in front of company personnel made her uncomfortable, however, deceiving Dante's family that evening was pure torture. They were all so delighted for her, so generous in their loving acceptance, so eager to help make her wedding day beautiful and memorable.

Not by so much as a glance did anyone hint disapproval at her condition or question the wisdom of so speedy a marriage. Dante had chosen her and that was enough. They welcomed her into their family without reservation.

She should have been reassured, the burden of her deceit made lighter. They knew Dante so much better than she did, after all, so they'd surely sense if his heart wasn't at least a little bit engaged. Instead she felt herself sinking into a quicksand of lies which grew more treacherous by the minute.

"How can we help you?" his sisters asked. "Tell us what we can do to make your wedding day wonderful. And you, too, Mrs. Connors-Lee. It's the bride's mother's privilege to share this time with her daughter and we don't want to intrude, but there isn't much time to arrange everything so, if you need us, we'd love to be involved."

Maeve spoke up then. "And we'd love to take you up on the offer, wouldn't we, Leila?"

"Oh, please! I need all of you," she told the table at large, but her gaze fastened on Dante.

"She does," he said, the very picture of tender concern. "Pregnancy's taking a toll on her energy and I don't want her too worn out to enjoy her honeymoon."

"Irene," her mother said, turning to Mrs. Rossi,

"you've already orchestrated five successful weddings, so I'll bow to your experience. What would you suggest…?"

It was all the encouragement needed. By the time dessert was served, ideas were flying with typical Rossi efficiency. The mothers had their heads together deciding on the guest list. Stephanie and Christine bickered over the best place to hold a reception. Annie promised to look after the flowers. Julia's husband, Ben, volunteered to walk the bride down the aisle.

Fuelled by such enthusiasm, the wedding took on a momentum of its own, a juggernaut of an affair plowing relentlessly forward regardless of any obstacles appearing in its path.

Stop! Leila silently cried out. *Everything's running out of control. It doesn't matter where or even if we have a reception. Who cares about the kind of flowers I choose or how many tiers there are to the cake? This isn't about a wedding day, it's about the marriage that comes after and mine promises to be empty of anything but mistrust and hurt.*

But no one heard her and the little she'd eaten at dinner threatened to rise up in protest. Mindful of her doctor's orders to avoid stress and very much aware of Dante eyeing her across the table, she sipped at her glass of ice water and willed the nausea to subside.

"We can be a bit overpowering once we sink our teeth into a project," Ellen, the most placid of Dante's sisters murmured, touching her arm sympathetically. "Are you having second thoughts about letting us get involved?"

"Not in the least. I'm truly grateful you're all so willing to lend a hand." She sipped again at the water. "I don't have the energy to put an afternoon tea party together these days, let alone a wedding."

"Have you thought about what you're going to wear?"

Given the state of affairs between her and Dante, it

occurred to Leila that black might be an appropriate choice but to have said so to one of his sisters would have been to contravene the terms of their contract. Instead, she said, "My waistline's expanding so rapidly, it'll have to something loose and fairly simple."

"I'd be happy to go shopping with you, Leila. Perhaps we can make a day of it, if you wouldn't find it too tiring, and go for lunch in the park."

"That sounds lovely," Leila said, "if you don't mind giving up a Saturday. I'm still officially on staff at Classic, even if all I'm really doing is making sure everything's in order for my successor to take over."

"Do you really think I'm going to let you work until your wedding day?" Dante said, plying her with another dose of affianced concern. "Sweetheart, Gavin's already got a list of applicants lined up for interview and until we make a final choice, we'll manage without you. I don't want you overtaxing your strength."

You don't want me around any more than you can help it, she thought wretchedly. The less you see of me, the better.

She had not thought her unhappiness showed but a few days later while they were taking a break from dress shopping, Ellen surprised her.

"You know, Leila," she said, "my brother can be a bit overbearing at times. It comes, I guess, from his being the man of the house since he was sixteen and also from his success in business."

They were sitting at a quiet corner table in the atrium of The Teahouse in Stanley Park. Earlier, it had rained, a heavy downpour more characteristic of February than late April, with a cold wind blowing in from the west. As a result, the restaurant wasn't packed with the usual, heavy lunch-hour crowd, even though the storm had passed, leaving clear skies and calm seas behind.

Leila watched the freighters swinging idly at anchor

in English Bay, not sure how best to respond to Ellen's remark. "I suppose," she said carefully, "it's the only way to be if getting ahead is important."

"Dante has always wanted more than just to get ahead." Ellen nibbled daintily at her spinach and strawberry salad, then dabbed her mouth with her napkin. "He has to be the best. I remember when he was still in elementary school. He must have been about ten at the time because I was in grade one. Not only was he an A student, he was also taller than most boys his age and it was never enough that, when it came to sports, he could do better than his classmates.

"No, he had to compete against kids two or more grades ahead of him—and come in first! He had to run faster, play soccer better, hit a ball farther, than any of them. The shelves in his room were full of medals and cups and other awards that he'd won."

"Why are you telling me this, Ellen?"

Ellen gave her a very level look and said, "Because when I watch him with you, I can't help but think that he sees you as another trophy he's determined to win."

"Are you saying you think our marriage is a mistake?"

"Not at all! You're exactly the right woman for him. I think what I'm trying to suggest is that, if he seems driven at times or focused on priorities different from yours, don't be discouraged. He does love you, Leila, I'm certain of that. He hasn't been my brother for the last thirty-three years for nothing. I know him too well, better, perhaps, than he knows himself."

"Yet you sense flaws in our relationship, and you're right." Leila blinked and looked out at the freighters again.

"So there are problems." Ellen pushed aside her plate. "Would it help to talk?"

"No." Leila drew a shuddering breath. Dante would never forgive her if she confided in one of his family. "Thank you, Ellen, but I can't."

"In that case, I won't press you. But before we drop the subject, let me say this. I think he is embarrassed and ashamed that you became pregnant before you were married."

Stunned at such a blunt assessment, Leila gasped.

"Because," Ellen continued, reaching across the table to grip her hand, "he blames himself. Everyone else is allowed to screw up occasionally, but not Dante. His role, as he sees it, is to fix mistakes, not make them. To be in charge, especially of his own life. When he found out you were expecting a baby—babies!—he realized there were some things he couldn't control. He broke his own rules and he can't forgive himself."

"He's never embarrassed," Leila said, remembering the way he'd almost bragged to their colleagues about her condition.

"Of course he is, Leila. He just won't let it show. But he'll get over it. All you have to do, if you love him and want to make a life with him, is wait it out. He'll come around, you'll see."

"I hope you're right." She didn't attempt to hide the tears springing to her eyes.

Ellen patted her hand again. "I am," she said firmly. "In the meantime, don't let him take his frustration out on you. Fight for the things you want. He'll respect you for it."

"The man I met on Poinciana Island might have," Leila said, "but I can't seem to find him anymore."

"Dare to show him you love him," Ellen said, "and you'll find he isn't lost, just hiding. Now eat up. We've got a wedding dress to buy. Of those you looked at this morning, which one takes your fancy?"

She took Ellen's advice, clinging to it in the hectic days that followed. Not that Dante was difficult or unpleasant. On the contrary, when they were together, he was charm itself. The problem was, the only times they were to-

She'd looked him in the eye and, without flinching, replied, "But I'm not any woman. I'm the mother of your children, I love you, and I deserve better than to be treated as if I were some money-grubbing tramp you'd picked up in a bar. And if you were half the man you like to think you are, you'd have recognized the fact before now and there'd have been no need for this confrontation ever to have taken place."

"Let's see how long your righteous indignation lasts when the creditors come banging on your door again," he'd said.

But she'd covered that eventuality, too. The sapphires and other gems which her father had given her over the years were gone, along with the heirloom pieces she'd inherited from his mother. The seven carat pigeon's blood ruby pendant, the starburst diamond and emerald brooch, the heavy gold bangles and exquisite jade ring had fetched a good price, enough to pay off the last of the debts and still leave a little for expenses in the months to come.

"How could you bear to part with such treasures?" her mother had wept, when she'd told her. "They were all you had left of your father."

But in the end, selling her jewelery had been less painful than selling her self-respect.

He hadn't believed she'd do it. He *couldn't* believe it. Even when she threw the damned ring on the table as if it were contaminated, he'd been sure hers was nothing more than a grand gesture of defiance and that she'd back down.

He'd heard the ping as the elevator arrived at the penthouse level and he'd waited for her to knock again at his door because it was beyond the bounds of credibility that she'd actually walk out on him. A good five minutes had elapsed before he'd begun to suspect otherwise.

Now, thirteen hours later, it still hadn't fully sunk in.

gether was in the presence of others. The rest of the time, he was busy.

But, "Busy or not, Dante," she said, finally cornering him outside his office during the lunch break on the Tuesday before the wedding, "we're going to have to make a decision on where we're going to live and there's a house I'd really like you to see."

"This isn't a good time, darling," he said, no doubt tacking on the "darling" because Meg was at her desk and taking in every word.

Leila had had enough. "Honey," she said, deliberately choosing the endearment he frequently tossed at her with such unvarnished sarcasm, "we're getting married in four days. When *will* it be a good time?"

He sighed and rolled his eyes at Megan. "Henpecked already and not even at the altar, Meg! What's a guy to do?"

"Go look at the house, of course. Leila's right. You've got to live somewhere."

"Okay, okay." He bathed Leila in a smile that could melt stone. "We'll go shopping. When's my last appointment, Meg?"

"Four-thirty with Gary Jefferson from ARGO."

"Reschedule it for tomorrow. There." He turned to Leila, hands raised in surrender. "Satisfied?"

"Yes," she said. "I'll set up an appointment with the Realtor."

"Leave the address of the house with Meg and I'll meet you there." He bent and kissed her, a not-too-brief, not-too-prolonged touch on her mouth. "Now I've got to go. Try to get in a nap before then."

"You're so lucky," Megan breathed, once his office door had shut behind him. "Honestly, Leila, I've never seen a man so besotted with a woman as Dante is with you."

Appearances were deceiving, Leila could have said.

He'd make plans to fly to the moon rather than spend any time alone with her.

How long did he intend to keep it up?

With only four days to go before she became Mrs. Dante Rossi, it was time, she decided, that she found out.

CHAPTER NINE

DANTE arrived at the house just after four. She was in the dining room when she heard the car draw up and his footsteps ascending the steps to the front porch, and her heart faltered.

The conviction which had bolstered her courage earlier evaporated, along with the ludicrous notion that she could achieve through feminine wiles what she'd failed to accomplish through reason.

But it was too late to back out now. She'd set the stage and there was no time to hide the fact. He was inside the house, calling out, "Anyone home?"

"In here, Dante," she quavered, wishing she'd chosen something less blatantly seductive to wear. The neckline of her new lemon maternity sundress was too revealing, the hem showed too much leg. "First door on your right."

He came to a stop on the threshold. "Where's the sales agent?" he said, looking around suspiciously. "I didn't see another car outside."

Of course not. When the Realtor had offered to drive them to the house, she'd told him, "We'd like to inspect the place on our own—just take our time and have a really good look around without having to worry about keeping you from your next appointment. Then, if we decide it's what we're looking for, we'll give you a call."

As a ploy to get Dante alone, it had seemed brilliant strategy at the time.

"I'm afraid he couldn't make it," she said now, faced with no choice but to play out the lie, "so I picked up the keys and came out here in a taxi."

Dante backed away as if he'd just discovered a corpse in the middle of the floor. "Then why the hell didn't you phone and cancel, Leila, instead of wasting my time? We can't make an offer or close a deal if he's not here."

Marshaling her flagging courage, she grabbed his hand and, drawing him farther into the room, scolded, "Don't fuss about trivialities, Dante. Come and look at the view, instead. Isn't it stunning?"

Reluctantly, he allowed her to tow him around the elegant dining table to the long windows looking north-west across the inlet to the mountains. "Very nice," he said shortly, "but what's the point in getting all fired up about a place that's full of someone else's furniture? Unless the present occupants are prepared to move over-night, there's no way we could take possession before the wedding."

"We can if we want to," she said, slipping her hand in the crook of his elbow and leaning her bare shoulder against his arm in the closest she'd come to real physical intimacy with him in weeks. "The vendors have moved to Australia and these furnishings they left behind are included in the price. The house is empty, Dante. We could move in tomorrow if we wished. Let me show you the other rooms."

"How many are there?"

"Four bedrooms with en suite baths upstairs, a den and family room on this floor as well as the main re-ception rooms and kitchen, and a games room down-stairs. Oh, and a conservatory off the breakfast nook and nanny quarters over the garage."

He seemed to notice how close they were standing then. Pointedly detaching himself from her clutches, he strolled through the butler's pantry to the kitchen. "Could you be happy living here?"

I could live in a shoe box and be happy if you were with me, she wanted to tell him, but it was too soon. His

guard was still up, invisible as a glass wall and just as
impenetrable. Perhaps later, if all went according to plan,
she could speak from the heart. For now, she contented
herself by replying in a tone which matched his in neu-
trality, "Yes. It's got the sort of space we need, certainly, and the location couldn't be better for you."

"Okay." He gave one of those indifferent shrugs that
had become his stock-in-trade of late. "We might as
well buy it then."

She hadn't allowed for such an eventuality. She'd
counted on his being too astute a businessman to commit
to such an investment without thoroughly checking it out
first. Dismayed, she said, "Don't you at least want to
look around before we decide that?"

"Why?" he said. "You're the one who'll be spending
most of your time here. If you're happy with it, that's
good enough for me."

"Well, it shouldn't be," she said, perversely changing
her mind about sabotaging her game plan when the
chance presented itself. "I like the looks and layout of
the house itself well enough, but I don't know anything
about plumbing and wiring, or termites and rotting
eavestroughs. What if the roof's ready to spring a leak
or the heating's inadequate?"

With ill-concealed impatience he shot back his cuff
and made no secret of the fact that he was checking his
watch. "What the hell, you're probably right. The rest
of the day's a write-off now anyway, at least as far as
getting any work done. Okay, let's begin with the outside."

A regal old dowager of sixty years, the house sat in
the seclusion of a garden awash with the scent of lilacs
and lilies. Clematis spangled a pergola with pale pink
flowers. A willow leaned gracefully over a small reflect-
ing pool one end of which was filled with water irises.
Dense holly hedges and a high brick wall screened the
entire property from passersby.

Except for the foundation which was stone, the exterior of the house itself was stucco painted a rich cream. Beveled glass panels in the long elegant windows trapped the sun's rays in rainbow prisms of color. A flight of steps led up to a graceful porticoed entrance.

After a thorough inspection of both the house and the grounds, Dante dusted off his hands and nodded approval. "This place'll outlive us, no question about that. It's built like a bunker. But I'm surprised you've chosen something this old. I expected you'd want something more up-to-date."

"I did look at quite a few new houses," Leila said, "but they didn't have the character or charm of this place and the lots were so small that one family could look right into the next door garden. I don't know about you, Dante, but I value my privacy too much to want our neighbors watching all our comings and goings."

"I agree. Yet even with so much land, it's safe enough for children to play outside here." He indicated the security system wired to the remote-controled wrought-iron gates leading to the road. "No unsavory characters'll be able to trespass on the property without our knowing. You say there are four bedrooms upstairs?"

"Yes."

"Lead on, then, and let's have a look at them."

Realizing that the moment of truth was almost upon her left her skin clammy and her voice breathless with nervous tension. "Um, yes...all right."

"You feeling sick again?" he asked, noticing her discomposure.

Oh, yes! Sick with hope and trepidation and longing! "A little," she improvised, leading the way inside quickly, before her courage deserted her completely. "I think it might be the sun. It's so hot out here."

She showed him the guest suite first. High-ceilinged with ornate crown molding like the rest of the rooms, it was spacious and airy, with upholstered window seats affording a fine view of the front lawns and rose garden. "Hmm," he said, clearly impressed. "Not too shabby by anyone's standards, I have to admit."

"And this one," she said, leading him into one of the two back rooms overlooking the rear garden and the inlet, "I thought would make a wonderful nursery. It's next door to the master suite and big enough for two babies, at least for the first couple of years."

He stuffed his hands in his pockets and gazed around. "I guess so. It's got plenty of cupboard space which is something my sisters always set great store by."

"That leaves us a spare room a bit smaller than the guest room…"

"Uh-huh."

"…And…" She gulped, afraid she might indeed throw up. At the far end of the hall, the double doors of the master suite loomed, more terrifying suddenly than the gates of hell. Quickly, before she turned tail and ran, she flung them wide. "…The main bedroom."

He paused in the doorway, his face unreadable.

She had set the scene with care. There were roses in a crystal vase on the nightstand, and chilled champagne. The gauzy white drapes at the open windows billowed slightly on the evening breeze, their undulations sensuous as a woman stripping for her lover.

Washed by the afternoon sun, the mahogany furniture flowed with subdued fire. The spires of the four-poster bed cast delicate shadows on the wall. Pillows plump with goose down and covered with cotton slips piled high against the headboard.

"What the hell is this?" Dante said softly.

She could not answer for the lump of sheer terror in her throat. She had thought to seduce him here, to revive for both of them the miracle they had found on Poinciana. But, like a rabbit trapped in the headlights of a speeding car, she froze, at a loss to know how best to proceed.

Should she sink down among the pillows with a come-hither look? Lure him by wantonly stripping off her clothes? Offer herself naked in all her thirteen-week pregnant glory and hope he wasn't repelled by the sight of her distended waist and swollen breasts?

Embarrassment burned her face. If her life depended on it, she could not. *Could not!* Whatever had made her believe she could?

"Leila?"

Dare to show him you love him, Ellen had urged and, foolishly, Leila had acted on the advice, believing she had nothing to lose.

But, except for her babies, nothing worth having if he refused her, she realized too late after the fact. No passion, no desire, no deep, abiding joy. Could she afford such a gamble?

But she'd gone too far to back out now, so she went to him and wound her arms around his neck. "This is for us, Dante," she said. "This is our room."

Although she felt rather than heard the swift intake of his breath, she knew she'd taken him by surprise. "Look," he said, grasping her shoulders and holding her at arm's length. "I don't know what you're trying to pull off here, Leila, but pretending we're your average bride and groom who are convinced marriage is one long bed of roses just isn't going to cut it."

"What is, then?" she murmured, leaning forward to press her lips to his throat. "Growing further apart with every passing day? How have we managed that, Dante? How did we manage to kill the love we once shared?"

He swallowed. "We struck a deal that had nothing to do with love and everything to do with expediency."

She strung a row of kisses along his jaw to his ear. "Why can't we have it both ways, Dante?"

"I make it a practise never to get personal with a business partner," he said, his voice textured with gravel.

Dare to show him....

"It's too late for that, Dante," she whispered, tracing the curve of his earlobe with the tip of her tongue. "We've been personal ever since the day we met."

His hands, which had grown slack at her shoulders, slid down her spine to clench at her waist. "Jeez," he muttered hoarsely.

It wasn't much encouragement but beggars couldn't afford to be choosy, and heaven knew, she was begging shamelessly. Nesting her hips against his groin, she said, "I made up the bed with linens from the bridal shower your sisters threw for me. Don't you think it would be a terrible waste not take advantage of them?"

"Cut it out," he said, but his flesh betrayed him and the sweat suddenly beading his forehead had nothing to do with the room temperature.

Undeterred, she drew down his head until his mouth hovered so close to hers that she could almost taste him. "It's been a long time since you kissed me as if you meant it, Dante."

"I've kissed you," he said, sounding like a man in pain.

"But not like this."

Deftly, she skimmed his lower lip with her tongue.

"For crying out loud, Leila, will you stop?" Fending her off, he loosened the knot in his tie and released the top button of his shirt, backing away from the bed as he did so.

But she could not stop. She could not ignore the cravings he aroused in her. She was on fire for him; aching and swollen and damp with desire. And he could deny until judgment day that he didn't feel the same, but the evidence was there for her to see. "It wasn't so very long ago that you'd have welcomed any excuse to touch me," she murmured, following him.

"Which is precisely how we got ourselves into the mess we're in now," he said, holding his shoulders very erect as if he hoped she wouldn't then notice that other parts of him were similarly afflicted. ''What the hell's gotten into you, Leila?''

Not you, she could have wept, *though there was a time that you'd have taken me anywhere, anytime.* But trying to convey her despair with words was impossible. Instead, helplessly, she approached him again and leaned against him in brazen, unmistakable invitation.

Even fully clothed, the feel of him, hard against her belly, was intoxicating. Aching for his touch, for a glimmering of the hunger he'd once shown for her, she lowered one strap from her shoulder and, taking his hand, drew it down her bare skin toward her breast. ''Dante,'' she pleaded.

Still he would not surrender.

Panic and passion converged on her then, choking her. Blindly her mouth sought the unyielding angle of his jaw, found his lips and would not let them go.

At first he continued to resist. But then, just when she was ready to concede defeat, a miracle occurred. The spark which no amount of mistrust or alienation had quite managed to douse flared into life again.

Crushing her to him, he kissed her back. Kissed her as he had not in days, with an anguish that drained her soul and left her mouth swollen and tender.

With one hand at her buttocks, he imprisoned her against him, pelvis to pelvis and nothing but a few layers of cloth to prevent him from driving into her. The other he fastened in her hair, so firmly that even if she'd wished, she could not have escaped the onslaught of that kiss.

But a flame so bright and hot could hurt as well as heal. Realizing he was courting destruction of all those defenses he'd so painstakingly built, Dante struggled to uphold them. ''Don't do this, Leila,'' he said harshly, wrenching his mouth away. ''The wedding's taking place on Saturday and I'll be there, as per our agreement. You don't have to act the whore to get me to the altar.''

Shock left her almost reeling. "Is that what you think this is all about, Dante?''

He gestured at the roses, the champagne, the marriage bed: all those witnesses to what she'd hoped would prove to be both a reconciliation and a new beginning. "What else? Or are you going to pretend these, too, were left behind by the previous occupants?''

"No," she whispered, strangling a sob. "I did all this. For us, Dante. I thought, if we made love again, if I showed you how much I need you and miss you, that we'd find our way back to each other. Otherwise, what's the point in our going on?''

The thud of a car door closing floated through the house. "We both know the answer to that, Leila," he said, shrugging his jacket into place and striding to the guest room window which looked down on the front entrance. "I'm the father of the twins you're expecting and you need money. I'm willing to pay off your mother's debts and offer you the respectability that comes of being Mrs. Dante Rossi, as well as honor my responsibilities to my children.''

"And what do you expect to get out of such an arrangement, Dante?''

"From a social and professional standpoint, it's time I acquired a wife, and whatever else your shortcomings, I'd be the last to deny that you're an enviable accessory to success. All I ask is that you maintain the image such a role requires. In short, we've arrived at an agreement in which we both come out winners. I believe in the old days it was called a marriage of convenience, one based on considerations other than love—and don't ask me to define what *that* is because I'm no longer sure I know.''

"It's being close to someone," she said, following him and plucking at his sleeve to try to detain him. "It's going to sleep in that person's arms at night and feeling as if you own the whole world. It's making love because you can't help yourself, because not to be intimate with your mate is a deprivation neither the soul nor the body can survive. I learned all that on Poinciana and try though I might, I can't forget it. I don't think you can, either, Dante. Am I mistaken?''

"A hell of a lot has happened since then, sweet face."

"Too much for us to regain what we once had?"

"Look," he said, swiping at his forehead with the back of his hand, "if you're asking me if I still want you, the answer's yes. I can't concentrate on a god-damned thing in the office for wanting you. I'm tired of taking cold showers and working till I'm ready to drop, just to get a decent night's sleep uninterrupted by dreams of how you feel under me when you reach orgasm."

As if beset by more devils than any mere mortal could be expected to withstand, he spun around suddenly and, grabbing a fistful of the bodice of her dress, hauled her close. "That car we heard a moment ago belongs to the real estate broker. Apparently he was able to make it here after all. But if I thought sex would fix what's broken between you and me, I'd leave him to cool his heels on the front doorstep and screw you right here, right now, until you begged me to stop."

"Dante!"

"But that wouldn't fix anything, would it, Leila?" he continued, ignoring her shocked exclamation. "Having you welcome me into your lovely body wouldn't alter the fact that you've never really allowed me inside your mind."

"How long are you going to punish me for misleading you?" she cried, devastated by his reaction. "Or are you saying there's nothing I'll ever be able to do to reestablish your trust in me?"

"Misleading me? Hell, Leila, you deliberately kept the truth from me on more than one occasion, first about Fletcher, then about your father, and let's not forget your pregnancy. But what really sticks in my throat is that, in each instance, you had plenty of opportunity to come clean before I found you out but you chose to keep quiet. So don't ask whether or not I'll ever trust *you* again because the way I see it, the problem is that you've never trusted *me*."

"How can you say that? I'm marrying you on Saturday."

"Yeah, well, I've always believed money can buy just about anything, and that's one truth you've certainly substantiated."

Too numb with pain and disappointment to answer, she simply stared at him.

Misconstruing her silence he released her. "Apparently we're in accord at last," he said, straightening his tie and buttoning his jacket. "So, on the strength of such a premise, I propose we go down and make a deal with that broker—unless, of course, your interest in this house only went as far as trying to get me in the sack?"

"No," she said, furious with herself for allowing desperation to coerce her into the kind of games she'd have refused to countenance when she was young enough to be forgiven for indulging in them. What had become of her self-respect, her dignity? "I like the house very much. But you're so eager to look for ulterior motives on my part that I'm beginning to think it doesn't matter what I say or do anymore."

"You've got a lifetime to prove me wrong, honey," he said, taking her elbow and steering her toward the stairs.

"Well, hello there!" The sales agent heralded their appearance with practiced bonhomie. "I stopped by on my way home on the off chance that you might still be here. So, tell me, now that you've had a good look at it, have you decided to snap up this fabulous chunk of real estate before someone else beats you to it, or what?"

''We're prepared to make an offer.'' Without missing a beat, Dante swung into action on what he did best: talking business and dealing figures.

Had he really kissed her so thoroughly just a few minutes ago that she'd thought her knees would give way? Leila wondered, watching from the sidelines. Had he once looked at her as if she were the only woman on earth who could make him forget himself so far that nothing mattered except that they be together, and to hell with wagging tongues? Most of all, would he ever look at her that way again?

The doorbell rang shortly after eight on Friday night. Since Maeve and Cleo had gone for their evening walk some half hour earlier, Leila assumed they'd forgotten their key again and hurried to answer.

But it was Anthony waiting on the step. Even though they'd talked on the phone and she'd invited him to the wedding, she hadn't seen him in weeks and noticed the change in him at once. The old Anthony was back, tanned and healthy-looking. ''Hope I haven't come at an inconvenient time,'' he said, following her into the parlor and placing a beautifully wrapped package on the coffee table. ''I know you've probably got a dozen last-minute things to attend to but I wanted you to have this before tomorrow. It's your wedding gift.''

''Why, thank you! But you didn't need to make a special trip out here tonight. You could have brought it with you to the church.''

''I'm afraid I won't be at the church, or the reception, either,'' he said, taking a seat beside her on the sofa.

''Oh, Anthony, why not? I have so few friends in town, I was really counting on your being there.''

''I'm flying to Europe first thing in the morning to see my nurse. She's got a week's leave and I'm meeting her in Vienna. As for my being at your wedding, it shouldn't matter how many friends show up for you, as long as the man you love is there.''

When she didn't answer but looked away instead, he took her chin in his hand and turned her to face him, his eyes mirroring concern. ''Is everything okay, Leila?''

''Yes.''

''You don't sound too sure.''

''I guess I'm feeling a bit overwhelmed. It's been so hectic, organizing a wedding in such a short time and, to top things off, we finalized the purchase of a house this afternoon.''

''And you're not happy about that?''

''Yes. It's a lovely place and we'll be able to take possession immediately.''

Anthony braced his hands on his knees and leaned forward. ''But something's wrong.''

She opened her mouth to deny the allegation and to her horror, burst into tears instead.

''Good God!'' he said. ''What is it? Tell me.''

''Nothing.'' She covered her face with both hands to stifle the sobs—a useless gesture because they kept coming anyway. ''Really, it's nothing. Just jittery nerves and exhaustion.''

He stroked her back as if he were comforting a child and when at last she gained control again, said, ''You know, I'll never forget the night you told me you'd met Dante. It was raining and blustery outside and I was feeling pretty low, what with one thing and another, but you lit up that room with sunshine, you were so happy. Where's it gone, Leila? What's happened to drive away that glow?''

''In case you haven't notice, I'm pregnant,'' she blurted out because, of all the problems facing her, that was the only one she felt she could confide to him. ''With twins.''

''Oops!'' he said. ''That must have come as a bit of a shock. But you're surely not sorry?''

"No. I always hoped I'd have children someday."

"And Dante? Is he happy?"

Her lip quivered embarrassingly. "I don't know what's going on in Dante's head these days. We're both so busy planning a future together that we don't have time for the present anymore. Sometimes I look at him and...and I see a stranger I'll be marrying on Saturday."

At first, Anthony didn't reply. He fished a clean handkerchief from the breast pocket of his blazer and handed it to her. At length, he said, "You know, in this day and age, Leila, people don't 'have to get married.' It's socially acceptable to be a single parent. So don't let yourself be pressured into going through with a wedding you're not ready for."

"I really don't have any choice, Anthony."

"You always have a choice." He looked at her thoughtfully and cleared his throat before going on. "At the risk of being indelicate, may I say that if money is an issue, I'd be more than happy—"

Good grief, if Dante ever knew that the subject had even arisen! "No, Anthony! Thank you very much, but no! Regardless of how I feel about Dante—and for the record, I do love him, very much—I couldn't possibly accept that kind of help from you."

"Why not?" he said. "It's only money and what use is it if it can't help out in a pinch?"

"You're very sweet and dear, Anthony."

"I'm also your friend," he said, "and the fact that you're marrying Dante isn't going to change that."

"I know." She managed a smile. "And that said, let's talk about your plans. Tell me how you found your nurse."

"I traced her through some contacts I have in the diplomatic corps. We exchanged a couple of letters, then, last week, we actually spoke by phone."

Leila thought she'd managed to steer the conversation away from her and Dante. While Anthony talked about

his lady, she opened his gift, exclaiming with genuine
delight at the exquisite Baccarat stemware he'd chosen.

Not until he rose to leave did he mention the wedding
again, and then only obliquely. "If you should find," he
said, "that you need to get away and be by yourself for
a while to sort things out, we have a place on Hernando
Island, up near the entrance to Desolation Sound. My
folks often go up there on long weekends, but there's a
guest house down near the water that stands empty and
is quite separate from the main lodge. All you'd have to
do is pick up the key from the caretaker's cottage."

Reaching up, she kissed his cheek. "Please don't
worry about me, Anthony. I wouldn't be marrying Dante
if I didn't truly love him and believe I can make him
happy. But thank you, all the same."

"Maybe you should consider how happy he can make
you, Leila. Because praiseworthy though it might be,
selfless devotion on one person's part can do only so
much. It takes two to make a marriage work, as you
quite rightly pointed out to me not so very long ago."

Leila gazed blankly at the darkened ceiling above her
bed. In the room next to hers, Cleo snored lustily but
Maeve's room, across the hall, was silent. Downstairs,
the mantel clock struck eleven. In one hour's time it
would be her wedding day. Twelve hours from now she
would become Mrs. Dante Rossi.

Her glance swung to the back of the door where her
wedding dress, cut along Empire lines and made of silk
crepe a shade lighter than Dante's eyes, hung from a
hook; to the hat and gloves on the dressing table, and
the pale kid shoes nestled in their tissue-lined box near
the stool.

"You'll look enchanting," Ellen had said, the day
they chose the dress. "Aquamarine is your color, Leila.
Dante won't be able to take his eyes off you."

Not so, Leila thought, throwing back the covers and

going to stand at the open window. She could show up wearing sackcloth and he wouldn't notice.

A soft breeze whispered over her, ruffling from her breasts to her abdomen, a ghostly reminder of the times when Dante had found her body fascinating enough to explore it at erotic, delicious leisure.

What would it take for him to turn to her again, to pledge himself to her, body and soul? A wedding ring? A signed marriage certificate?

He touched her clear through to her soul but, if she couldn't reach him, could she settle for being the adored corporate wife in public, and the shunned in private?

The questions attacked without mercy, offering no answers and oppressing her beyond endurance.

A woman's wedding should be a time of excitement and joyful anticipation, not an occasion filled with fear and uncertainty. No bride should be walking the floor hours before she said "I do," questioning whether or not she had the stamina to survive living with her husband. And no marriage should be expected to thrive in an atmosphere of doubt and mistrust.

"I cannot go through with this," she whispered to the quiet night, the tears flooding her eyes and rolling down her face. "I cannot marry Dante."

CHAPTER TEN

NINE hours, two bus rides and two ferry trips after she said goodbye to her mother and Cleo, Leila sat aboard the water taxi taking her on the last leg of her journey to Hernando.

As dusk deepened into night, the island rose ahead, a shadowy hump dotted with occasional lights etched against the darker bulk of the mainland mountains. Apart from the muted growl of the water taxi's engine, the air was still, the sea calm as glass except for the delta of ripples caused by the boat's passage.

"Almost there, miss." The skipper cut the throttle and pointed to the left. "You can see the light at the end of the Fletcher dock about a hundred yards to port."

The morning seemed a lifetime ago. She'd left the house early, arriving at Dante's apartment shortly after eight-thirty. From there, she'd gone to the bank and then to an estate jeweler. When she'd eventually returned home, her mother and Cleo were hovered together at the front door, fluttering with agitation.

"Leila, darling!" her mother had exclaimed, hurrying down the path to meet her. "Where in the world have you been? When we brought you breakfast in bed and found you weren't there, we didn't know what to think, did we, Cleo? And we've been frantic ever since."

"The child had her reasons," Cleo declared. "I told you, Maeve, that I foresaw trouble. Look at her face now, then dare to tell me again that you think I'm a fool to believe in the cards."

"What happened, Leila?" Features drawn with worry,

her mother knotted her hands at her throat. "Where have you been?"

"I went to see Dante."

"My heavens, don't you know it's bad luck for the groom to see his bride before the wedding?"

"There isn't going to be a wedding," Leila had said, regretting that she couldn't break the news more gently. But this was one truth that couldn't be dressed up to make it appear less than it was. "I've broken things off with Dante."

"Ah," Cleo proclaimed sagely, trailing in her wake as she walked into the house. "As I predicted, the storm has broken."

Maeve hadn't been so easily dissuaded. "Of course there's going to be a wedding," she'd said, darting ahead of them. "It's twenty past ten already and you're due at the church in an hour, so forget this silly attack of last-minute stage fright and start getting ready. You'll be fine once you step into your dress."

"Didn't you hear me, Mother? I'm not getting married today."

"But, darling, you have to! Guests are arriving at the church even as we speak."

"I'm afraid they're in for a disappointment."

That she meant what she said finally had sunk home. "Have you lost your mind?" Maeve gasped, throwing up her hands in horror.

"No. I've come to my senses." Strangely calm, Leila sat down at the table, buttered a piece of cold toast and began eating. For the first time in weeks, she'd found each mouthful delicious.

"Unless I've sadly underestimated him, I can't imagine Dante letting you get away with this."

"Short of hog-tying me and dragging me to the altar, there's not a whole lot he can do to prevent it, Mother."

Dazed, her mother had sunk into a chair. "What

brought on this sudden change of heart? I thought he was the love of your life, just as your father was mine.''

''He was and probably always will be. But I've come to realize that love by itself isn't necessarily enough to keep a marriage afloat.''

''It was for your father and me. It carried us past all the rough spots.''

''Not when it really counted, it didn't. Or did it never occur to you to question why he didn't stick around and face up to his troubles, instead of taking the easy way out and leaving you to deal with them?''

''He was too ashamed. He thought he'd let me down. He died a broken man.''

''He was a coward, Mother.''

''Shame on you, Leila! How could you say such a thing?''

''And Dante is a bully,'' Leila had continued, unperturbed. ''If I'm going to promise before God to love, honor and cherish a man for the rest of my life, I'd prefer him to be somewhere between the two extremes.''

''You *have* lost your mind!'' her mother practically whimpered.

''She's making perfect sense to me,'' Cleo said.

''How would you know? You've never been in love, Cleo. You can't begin to understand.''

Surprisingly, Cleo had said, ''I was in love once, but the gentleman in question turned out to be most undeserving of my affections. If Leila has reached the same conclusion about her intended, it's not up to you to try to change her mind.''

Maeve had dismissed the observation much as one would swat at a fly. ''Rubbish! Leila, darling, I'm begging you to reconsider. It's not too late—a phone call is all it would take.''

''No, Mother.''

''Dante's a proud man, Leila. Humiliate him like this

in front of his family and friends, and he won't easily forgive you."

"If I don't take a stand now, I'll never forgive myself."

"But what about the babies? My goodness, if you won't think of yourself, think of them. Do you want them to grow up not knowing their father?"

Leila had polished off a second piece of toast before saying, "No more than I want them growing up in an atmosphere of resentment and strife, which is what I'd be subjecting them to if I went ahead with the marriage at this time. Dante isn't ready to be a husband."

"But he loves you, Leila."

"Yes," Leila had conceded sadly. "In his own way, I think he does. The trouble is, he really doesn't like me very much, Mother. And I don't hold out much hope for love to survive in that kind of climate."

She'd made the right choice, she assured herself, climbing from the water taxi onto the dock. In fact, she'd made the only choice. But that was cold comfort to a breaking heart. Right up until she'd exited his building and stepped into the waiting cab, she'd prayed Dante would come after her.

It would have taken so little to make things right. All he'd have had to do was take her in his arms and tell her his real reason for wanting to marry her was that he loved her and needed her. She'd have believed him. She'd have believed he could walk on water if only he'd shown her a fraction of the tenderness he'd once showered on her.

But he had not. His initial disbelief and anger had sunk into frozen sullenness. His eyes, which once had reminded her of a sunlit tropical lagoon, had resembled a northern lake in the grip of winter: bleak, icy, dead. As dead as she wished she could be.

She would have to write to his mother, she thought, following a gravel path from the water and up past a large log house to where lights shone from the windows of a cottage near the road. At the very least, she owed Mrs. Rossi an apology, even if she couldn't offer an explanation. Because how did one tell a mother that, when it came to the crunch, her son simply hadn't measured up?

And his sisters...she'd grown so fond of them. Their support and affection had meant more to her than they could begin to guess. Would they ever forgive her for the hurt she'd dealt to their family?

As she approached the cottage, a man of about fifty whom she correctly assumed to be Dale, the caretaker, appeared from the back. "You should have phoned and let me know you were coming up," he scolded, when she explained why she was there. "I'd have opened the place up and aired it out a bit. It hasn't been used since last summer. Here, let me carry that bag and see you settled in for the night. The cupboards and freezer are always kept well stocked, so you won't starve, but I'll need to turn on the water."

At any other time, she'd have found the guest house charming, with its deep decks overlooking the Sound on three sides and a great stone fireplace filling one entire wall of the living area. Paneled in pine, with wide plank floors and chintz-covered sofas grouped around the hearth, it exuded warmth and welcome.

"If it's peace and quiet you're looking for," Dale said, hauling in a fresh load of logs and setting a match to the kindling already stacked in the grate, "you've come to the right place. 'Less I hear from you, I won't come bothering you and neither will the missus. But if there's something you need, don't hesitate to holler. That's what I get paid for. Oh, and before I forget, you'll notice a hot tub on the deck outside the bedroom. I just turned the heater on but it'll likely take an hour or so before it's up to speed. Otherwise, the place is ready to go."

After he'd gone, she was completely alone for the first time since she'd told Dante she was calling off the wedding. Alone with the memory of that meeting and unable to escape the terrible, gaping wound she'd inflicted on herself by taking such action.

She had walked away from the father of her children; from the man who, even locked in a disbelieving rage aimed solely at her, still held the power to storm her heart with a glance, a touch.

"Don't try playing this eleventh hour game with me, Leila," he'd said flatly, when she'd told him her intentions, "because I won't let you get away with it. You'll be there at the church as planned."

He'd been out running along the beach in the park earlier and was wearing shorts and a T-shirt. Still unshaven and with his hair curling damply at the ends, he looked less like a high-powered CEO than a lifeguard—if one discounted the voice, sharp with authority, and the fire in his eyes.

"I'm afraid not," she'd said, knowing that either she stood her ground now or spent the rest of her life letting him get away with one ultimatum after another.

He'd faced her, his long, smoothly tanned legs planted firmly apart as if, by the sheer force of his will, he could stop the earth from turning if he chose, and laughed at her. "Of course you will, honey," he said scornfully. "You don't have any choice, remember?"

For the first time, she'd known real anger toward him. "I will not prostitute myself for anyone, not even you, Dante," she'd told him, dropping her engagement ring onto a brass tray on the coffee table. When she walked out of his door, he'd turned away and stared out of the window rather than watch her go.

Where was he now? Alone like her, pacing the floor of his living room, and wondering how they'd come to such a pass? Drowning his sorrows in Scotch and reviling her for the public embarrassment she'd caused him?

Had he gone to the church himself and sent everyone home or designated the job to an underling?

Restlessly, she stepped out onto the deck. The moon had risen in the southeast, so full it cast shadows and flooded the bay with light. A sloop rocked gently at the end of a pier farther down the beach. Somewhere behind the guest house, a chorus of frogs serenaded the night.

If she had upheld her part of the marriage contract, she and Dante would be on their honeymoon now. Would wearing his wedding ring and taking his name have convinced him to treat her as his wife in every sense? Would she at this moment be lying in his arms, aglow in the aftermath of making love? Or would they merely have had sex, a cold and clinical exercise in passion without tenderness?

Almost sick with misery, she stared out at the nighttime brilliance of the bay and wished she could live the last three months over again and get it right this time.

Impatiently, she dashed at the tears blurring her vision and turning the moon to shattered silver. Dante was right. Sex had never been the problem between them, any more than it would have been the solution. The rift ran deeper than that.

Yet her connection to him remained strong. The fact of her pregnancy made it impossible to sever all their ties. When the pain became bearable, they would see each other again, exchange dialogue, even share time together because of their children. But she would never again turn to him for help.

"I'd like to think we'll work things out someday," she'd told him. "But I refuse to be a victim, Dante. I won't be browbeaten anymore, I won't tolerate your ultimatums, and I won't be blackmailed. So you'll have to come to me, with no strings attached."

"Don't hold your breath," he'd sneered. "It'll be a cold day in hell before I come crawling after any woman."

Oh, there was no doubt that this morning's fiasco had happened. He wasn't likely to forget in a hurry the humiliation of standing before the guests at the church and telling them to go home because the wedding had been canceled.

He hadn't been able to abide their sympathetic murmurs, even less their hushed deference as they filed out. As a point of pride, he'd remained in front of the altar until every last pew had emptied, grateful that he'd at least had time to prevent his mother and sisters from witnessing this, the ultimate indignity of his life.

Eventually, he'd driven over to face the family. They were all there in the house he'd grown up in, his nieces red-eyed with disappointment at not being flower girls after all and his mother still in tears. "How did this happen, Dante?" she'd sobbed. "What went wrong?"

They'd all clustered around him then, bolstering him with sympathy, offering support, assuring him that everything would eventually turn out okay, that being pregnant often made women do and say irrational things.

All, that was, except Ellen. "You boneheaded idiot, what did you do?" she whispered, dragging him unceremoniously out to the back porch and punching him in the shoulder. "How did you manage to louse up the best thing that's ever happened to you?"

"Shut up," he'd muttered, too taken aback that she, the most placid of his sisters, should be the one to turn on him with such spirit.

"I will not! You've been riding for a fall for a long time, Dante, so high on your success with Classic that you've started to believe the mythology of your own PR department. When did the brother I used to know become such an unfeeling, arrogant ass?"

"Standing by the woman carrying my children hardly strikes me as arrogant or unfeeling."

"Is that what this so-called marriage was all about?"

she'd spluttered, practically exploding with temper. "Your doing the right thing? Well, la-di-da! Where was all this high-minded morality when you…you *knocked her up?*"

"Careful, Ellen," he'd said. "Your blue collar background is showing."

She'd slapped his face then, winding up with a right-hander that had rocked him back on his heels. His cheek still bore the faint red imprint of her fingers. "You unspeakable, ignorant snob! Leila has more class in her little finger than you'll ever find in your whole oh-so-perfect body! She was right to dump you. With attitude like yours, she's better off alone."

"And my children?" With an effort, he'd contained his shock at this, the final betrayal. He'd always been sure he could count on every member of his family to take his side, no matter what.

"Oh, they won't be alone, Dante. They'll have a solid-gold mother who cares, and at least one aunt who'll be there for them, no matter how much their father manages to screw up."

"In case you haven't yet realized," he said, "I'm not the one who canceled out at the last minute. I was prepared to go through with the wedding and, for what it's worth, the marriage."

"Well, it isn't worth spit!" she snapped. "Because, in case *you* hadn't noticed, that woman loved you, though heaven knows why. She would have walked through fire for you, Dante."

"Apparently not, Ellen. When it came right down to what really counted, she was a no-show."

"And it's not yet occurred to you to wonder why, has it? You're so busy playing the injured victim that you've never once asked yourself what you did to provoke such action. Or do you think it's all in a day's work for a woman to call off her wedding at the last minute?"

"I don't pretend to understand how the female mind works."

"Well, start taking lessons. Because you've obviously got a lot to learn." She glared at him, but the fire in her eyes was dimmed by the sparkle of tears. "You're my brother and I love you," she wailed, collapsing against him. "I hate to see you hurting but damn you, you deserve it!"

"Don't cry," he said, slinging his arm around her. "Leila and I might still be able to work things out."

Ellen wiped her eyes on the end of his tie. "Will you go to her, Dante?"

Not on your life, he'd thought. Leila had been the one to walk away and she'd have to be the one to come back. "I'll think about it," he'd said.

"Anthony knows how you can get in touch with me, should you decide you want to try again," she'd told him, before she'd left him, knowing that, in bringing up Anthony's name, she ran the risk of alienating Dante forever.

But Anthony had shown himself to be a good friend, something Leila valued highly, and she'd refused to diminish his kindness to her just to cater to Dante's unfounded jealousy.

When she had fallen in love with Dante, it had been more than just his body that had stolen her heart. His strength of character had played their part, his integrity and inborn sense of fair play.

All she could do now was hope that, given time, those qualities would conquer his pride enough to allow him to come to her. For the first few weeks she clung to that belief so fiercely that she'd awaken each morning convinced that *this* would be the day. But as May slid closer to June and summer became a tangible presence rather than a promise, her hopes began to fade.

On the positive side, the clean, fresh air and peaceful

surroundings worked their magic. Her health improved dramatically. The nausea disappeared and with it the enervating fatigue that had made her first trimester so hard.

She spent hours walking along the shore, collecting shells, or reading from the vast collection of paperbacks in the guest house library. She began to enjoy meals again.

When he heard that she loved seafood, Dale kept her supplied with a variety of delicacies. Every few days, she'd find a pail of fresh clams on her doorstep, and she'd make a chowder that would see her through several dinners. Other nights she'd feast on oysters or salmon.

His wife, June, taught her to knit and she began making little things for her babies. Of an evening, she'd often wait until after sunset then spend an hour relaxing in the hot tub.

Gradually, her body recovered its former vitality. Her hair shone with health, her skin glowed. She slept long and well in the big sleigh bed with its soft, deep mattress. Too well, sometimes, when she'd dream of Dante so vividly that it broke her heart to wake up and find he was not there beside her.

She was at her weakest then, so vulnerable that the temptation to renege on her self-promise tore at her. *Go to him. Be the one generous enough to make amends,* her heart advised. She'd wander out onto the deck and watch the new day come alive but, while the world basked in sunshine, in her heart it was raining. At those times it seemed to her that it had been raining for weeks, a cold, gray relentless downpour that never abated.

Once she got as far as dialing his number, then hung up before it rang at the other end because she knew that it would resolve nothing. He had to want her badly enough that, this time, he'd come to her.

In her sixteenth week, she felt life stirring within her womb, tiny fluttering movements that brought the reality of her pregnancy home to her in a way that nothing else had. But her sense of wonder was tarnished by not being able to share the moment with Dante.

Twice she traveled to the mainland for medical check-ups at a clinic in Powell River, recommended by her doctor. She phoned her mother every Sunday. Cleo wrote to say the cards predicted she'd deliver identical twin boys three weeks ahead of schedule. Once, after his return from Vienna, Anthony flew up to spend the day with her and introduced her to the next-door neighbors, Lew and Claire Drummond, a couple in their early sixties who spent each summer at their island retreat.

But tranquillity and solitude could become too much of a good thing. She began to tire of her own company and when Claire took to inviting her over for morning coffee or afternoon tea and, occasionally, a beach barbecue, Leila found she was ready to interact with other people again.

One Friday evening near the middle of June, when she'd all but given up hope of finding her happy-ever-after ending with Dante, she was invited to a cocktail reception marking an annual Drummond tradition. Friends from as far back as college days came from all over the lower mainland to celebrate the start of the summer season with a weekend of partying.

From early that morning, the boats had begun to arrive. By late afternoon a fleet of motor cruisers was moored at the dock while out in the bay several sailboats rode at anchor. When she arrived on the Drummonds' back lawn, shortly before seven, the party was in full swing.

"Come and meet people," Claire said, hurrying to greet her and drawing her into the crowd. "These are the Martins, Chad and Adrienne, who live at the other end of the island. And this is my nephew Max who's going to be a darling and get you something to drink.

She's pregnant, Max, so make it nonalcoholic. Oh, and Leila, I want to be sure to introduce you to…''

The names flowed past her, too many to remember. Max pressed a tall cool glass of sparkling grape juice into her hand. A woman asked her when her baby was due and backed away as if she was contagious when she said she was expecting two. Music spilled out of the house, old ragtime melodies played on a honky-tonk piano, underscored by the sound of laughter and animated conversation in the garden.

She was talking to a couple celebrating their twenty-fifth wedding anniversary when the float plane appeared from the south and circled over the bay. As the roar of its engine gradually drowned out the voices, everyone turned to watch its descent.

It skimmed the surface of the water about a hundred yards out, throwing up twin rooster tails of spray, then settled on its pontoons and taxied toward to the end of the dock.

Shading her eyes, Leila turned to watch like everyone else as a lone figure climbed out of the cockpit and leaped ashore. But while the buzz of curiosity indicated that he was a stranger to the others present, Leila was not deceived.

Although the sun rode low in the sky behind him, casting him in silhouette, she knew at once it was Dante. If there'd been a dozen men approaching, she'd have recognized the confident stride, the proud angle of the head, the lean-hipped elegance, that were his trademark.

She was not aware of pulling away from the other guests. She did not even know she was gravitating toward him as though pulled by some invisible magnet. Only when she felt the smooth, weathered wood of the railing beneath her hand did she realize she'd left the party behind and reached the ramp leading to the dock.

Vaguely she was aware of the slap of waves against the pilings, of the guests grown suddenly silent on the

Drummonds' lawn as they witnessed the scene unfolding in that long stretch of no-man's land connecting sea to shore.

At last he saw her, stopped dead and, for a small eternity, simply stood and looked at her. The canvas bag he held slung over one shoulder dropped to the boards with a thud she felt rather than heard. He wiped his palms down the sides of his denim-clad thighs. She saw his head go up, his shoulders straighten.

Apprehension rushed over her then. She'd waited forever for this moment, sure it could bring nothing but undiluted joy. Yet poised as she was at the top of the ramp, she felt exposed and defenseless, and very uncertain.

She wanted to run, to hide. The aftermath breeze of the departing float plane had plastered her maternity dress against her, detailing the changes pregnancy had wrought on her body. Nervously she plucked at the fabric, attempting to hold it away from her like a tent.

Even though a distance of some fifty yards or more separated them, she knew he saw how different she was from the woman who'd walked out on him on their wedding day. How, she wondered, the panic stealing her breath away and hammering at her heart, could he find her attractive still?

At length he moved, scooping up the bag and loping toward her until, at last, he was so close he could have touched her. But he did not. He merely towered over her, unbearably attractive, incredibly sexy and completely terrifying.

His gaze scoured the length of her, taking in her face, her throat, her breasts and coming to rest at last on the swell of her pregnancy.

She snapped under that slow, intense scrutiny. "Why are you here, Dante?" she said, and was appalled at the way her question emerged, peremptory and cold, as if he'd embarrassed her by gate-crashing the Drummonds' party when he knew full well he was the person she least wished to see.

She thought something flickered in his expression, something quick and pained, but he masked it so swiftly that she couldn't be sure. "I've come to set you free," he said, his voice flowing over her as darkly velvet as a summer's night. "Is there someplace private we can talk?"

CHAPTER ELEVEN

SHE didn't ask him to explain himself; didn't by so much as a flicker of expression betray whether or not she was glad to see him. All she did was nod calmly and turn back down the ramp, leaving him to follow at her heels like a whipped dog.

He hadn't counted on things happening quite that way. First, he'd hoped to take her by surprise in the cottage Fletcher had described to him. He'd wanted to reacquaint himself with the shape and texture of her—her skin, her hair, her unforgettable face.

He'd rehearsed exactly what he wanted to say, had visualized in his mind's eye how he'd present his case. The last thing he'd expected was that she'd be involved in some fancy shindig with a crowd of people from next door who'd decided to horn in on his act.

"Leila!" one of them screamed, waving furiously. "Bring your friend over and have him join the party."

"No goddamned way," he said, not giving her the chance to decide otherwise. "I didn't come all this way to make small talk with strangers."

She tilted her shoulder in a gesture of acquiescence and walked over to speak to the screamer who, by then, had been joined by a horde of other dressed-to-kill yachting types. He couldn't hear what excuse she offered for abandoning them but he hated watching her smile warmly at strangers when the best she could offer him was a guarded sort of reserve.

He knew he'd painted himself into a corner and deserved whatever punishment she chose to mete out. But reasonable or not, he wanted her smiling at him, telling him with her eyes that she couldn't wait to be alone with him. He wanted to say his piece and then, if she'd let him, he wanted to start over.

He wanted her in his bed, naked and flushed with passion. He wanted her sleeping next to him, with her belly propped against his spine. He wanted to feel their unborn children moving beneath his hand. Oh, God, he wanted—so badly he hadn't been able to function for the pain it brought him.

Balancing his bag on the ramp rail, he let his gaze roam over her, taking in the changes that had occurred in the month she'd been gone. She was still slender as a reed, so sweetly slender that there wasn't a part of her he couldn't cup in his hand—except for the swell of her pregnancy, much more pronounced now than it had been a month ago.

How could so delicate a frame possibly survive giving birth? What if the babies were built like him, with shoulders like a running back?

He looked away, ashamed and frightened. *Frightened....* The impact hit him like a fist smashed into his face. He hadn't been frightened since he'd been a child—until he met her. And since then, he'd been nothing *but* frightened.

"We can go up to the house now."

He hadn't noticed her come back. She stood at the foot of the ramp waiting for him, her animation again replaced by cool reserve.

"I'd like that," he said.

The cottage was comfortably luxurious without being in the least ostentatious, though why that should surprise him he couldn't fathom since he'd read everything else wrong where Anthony Fletcher was concerned. Solidly constructed, well appointed, and with nothing but great expanses of sea and sky beyond its windows, the place made an ideal retreat.

Leila's own touches added to the charm. A jug holding a bunch of wildflowers stood on the mantel. An open paperback lay facedown on the sofa, with some knitting beside it. At the end of the counter separating kitchen from living area was a bowl of shells.

"Did you collect these?" he asked, tracing his finger over the coils of an oyster drill.

"Yes. I love walking on the beach at low tide."

"And this place?" He jerked his head to encompass the house. "You're happy here?"

"For now," she said.

He waited for her to elaborate, to give him the opening he needed to say what had to be said. But she chose not to. Instead, she pulled out one of the chairs at the table, sat with her hands folded composedly in her lap, and left it up to him to carry the conversational ball.

"Yeah...well...." He cleared his throat, more than a little outraged to find himself pinned in a stranglehold of anxiety. "I guess you're wondering how I knew where you were?"

"I assume you phoned Anthony."

"Not exactly. I went to see him."

Her eyes widened. "You went to see him?"

"Yeah. It was no big deal."

"Really?"

Her skepticism shamed him into truth. "No," he admitted. "It was just about the toughest thing I've ever done, to go, cap in hand, and ask the man I perceived to be my rival if he'd help me find you."

"Yes," she said, her quiet dignity still intact. "I can imagine that it must have been."

Privately, he'd thought he deserved a medal for what he'd done, but if he found her matter-of-fact response somewhat underwhelming, he wasn't about to let her know. The time was long past when he could afford such petty self-indulgence, and Fletcher had been more than decent. "I expected he'd rub my nose in the fact that I was at the mercy of his generosity. I probably would have, if our positions had been reversed. But he just asked me, very civilly, why I wanted to find you.''

"And what did you say, Dante?"

Bracing himself, he met her steady gaze. "I told him that there were matters needing to be sorted out between you and me. He agreed.''

She looked down at that, and smoothed the palm of her hand over her belly. He found the gesture profoundly moving and erotic. "Was that all you talked about?" she said.

"Not quite." He swallowed another unpalatable chunk of hubris. "Just as I was leaving, he said that falling for a woman and being her lover was easy, it was being her friend that took work.''

She smiled then, a brief and lovely expression of fondness that fleetingly lit up the room. "That sounds like Anthony. He's a wonderful man.''

He ached to have her smile at him that way and had to swallow the surge of jealousy that rose in his throat. "Yeah, well, for what it's worth, I'm sorry I behaved like such an ass where he was concerned. You're not a bone to be fought over and carried off by the bigger, stronger dog and I had no business acting as if you were.''

"You're naturally competitive, Dante. It's as much a part of you as the color of your hair.''

"That's all very fine but when a man becomes too focused on winning to value the prize, his achievements are worthless. I wanted to possess you, to show the world that I'd got the woman no other man had managed to win. And I ended up with nothing.''

She pierced him with a look then, her eyes intolerably huge and solemn. "We made a dreadful mess of things between us, didn't we?''

"I certainly did, right down to letting a jerk like Newbury get to me." He could hardly speak for the lump in his throat. If he hadn't known better, he'd have thought he was close to breaking down and bawling. But it had been so long since he'd cried that he couldn't remember how anymore.

Pulling himself together, he went on. "By the way, he's no longer with the company. He got caught harassing a young woman in accounting and was given his walking papers. Not only that, his wife kicked him out, as well. Seems she decided she'd rather be on her own than put up with a guy like that—which brings me to what I really came here to say. You don't have to marry me, Leila. The blackmail's at an end. I've come to set you free. There'll be no more ultimatums, no more high-handed demands."

"Then what do you want, Dante?"

"To help you, not because I expect anything in return but because I love you. If I cannot be your husband, at least let me be your friend. The babies I will love because we created them together, because they will be all that is wonderful about you and, hopefully, the best that is in me. So let me give, for a change."

When she didn't answer, he spread his hands helplessly and struggled to find the right words. "I know it's not enough to say 'I love you,' that showing it is what counts. I know, too, that I screwed up royally but, if it's not too late, I'd like to try to make it up to you now."

"It wasn't all your fault," she choked, starting to cry herself. In the fading light, her eyes gleamed like beautiful deep-water pools ready to overflow. "I did my share of damage."

He'd promised himself he'd keep his distance at least until he'd said everything he came to say. But for the first time in weeks she was close enough to touch, and the sight of her distress was more than he could bear. "Oh, hell, Leila," he said hoarsely, reaching for her, "the last thing I want is to cause you any more pain."

She came into his arms and rested against him, her head tucked against his shoulder and her belly nestled between his hips. How was it possible, he agonized, that while their bodies had always found such a perfect fit, their minds had been out of kilter almost from the first?

"Don't cry," he begged, combing his fingers through her hair.

"I can't help it," she wept, her body shaking with sobs. "If I'd had more faith in you, I could have prevented so much heartache for both of us. But I wanted to teach you a lesson and we've both ended up paying for it. I humiliated you in front of everyone you care about, your family, your colleagues, your friends, and—"

"And I needed to be taught that lesson, sweetheart. I've been carrying a chip on my shoulder that's ruled my life for too long. Call it reverse snobbery or whatever you like, but for what it's worth, Leila, pride and success are cold bedfellows when they're all a man has left. There's nothing so glaringly clear as hindsight, and if I had it all to do over again, I'd go about it differently. Whatever else my failings, though, I do know when to quit and all I can say now is I'm sorry for having made you pay for my..."

He struggled briefly with himself, hating the word that came to mind but knowing of no other that would do. "...My insecurities. And to try in some small way to make up for what I've done."

Unwillingly, he let go of her and fished out the box he'd stashed inside his bag. Tipping out the contents on the table, he continued, "No one holds greater stock in family than I do, and these heirlooms didn't belong in a pawn shop."

"But they weren't" she said softly, staring down at the lovely, familiar pieces glimmering in the twilight. "They were in the hands of an estate jeweler."

"Same thing, different name. What matters is that now they're back where they belong."

"How did you know what I'd done?" she whispered, tears tracking silver down her cheeks again.

"I went to your mother to pay off her creditors. When she said you'd already taken care of them, I bullied her into telling me how."

"I can't let you do this, Dante. My father's debts aren't your responsibility."

"They're not yours, either." Aiming to lessen the tension, he tried for a laugh which fell sadly short of the mark. "If the thought of accepting charity from me sits ill with you, think of it as taking care of our children's inheritance."

She dipped her head in a gesture of acceptance. "Thank you."

Over the din of the party next door, he heard the roar of the Beaver plane returning. "You're welcome. And now that I've taken care of what I came to say and do, I'll leave you to your summer hideaway."

"But you can't leave now!" she exclaimed. "There's no way off the island until tomorrow."

"The pilot who brought me in had to make a delivery on Cortes. I arranged for him to pick me up on his way back to Vancouver."

He slung the empty bag over his shoulder and looked at her long and hard, committing to memory the sight of her every feature. "Take care of yourself, Leila, and of our babies. I won't bother you again but know that I'm only a phone call away if you need me. I've arranged for money to be deposited to your account, so you don't need to worry on that score."

"You don't have to do that," she protested.

"Yes, I do," he said. "I might have lost you, but I've still got to live with myself. And although we might not be a couple any longer, they *are* my babies you're carrying."

He wanted to kiss her before he left. Wanted it so badly that the pain almost crippled him. But he dared not. There'd never be a time when he could kiss Leila goodbye with any sort of equanimity.

So he lifted his hand in a salute and got the hell out of the house before she saw that his vision was blurred and he was choking on tears.

Blindly, he stumbled down the path and climbed the ramp. The Beaver was just nosing up to the end of the dock. Vancouver lay only an hour's flight away, but if it were half a world away, the pain of leaving her couldn't have been worse.

He felt empty inside. Used up. He had nothing of value to give anyone because he had no heart. He'd left it behind with her.

This time, he was the one walking away. Not in anger but in defeat. Her wounded lion no longer stalking proudly but limping with pain.

Horrified, she watched as his silhouette grew smaller against the crimson horizon, unable to believe that the fire and fury of their love had been reduced to this feeble submissive flicker.

She could not let it happen. He'd come to her and laid his heart at her feet and not asked for a thing in return. He had made it possible for them to forge a new kind of commitment to each other for their children's sakes. But romantic love, the kind that dreams were made of, was fragile as spun glass. If she let him go now, they would never repair the damage.

The realization spurred her to action.

"Wait!" she cried, her feet at last obeying the commands of her heart and propeling her out of the house and down the steps to the path. "Dante, come back!"

But her words were swallowed up by the music from next door and the idle of the float plane engine. He could not hear her. By the time she'd reached the top of the ramp, he was balanced on a pontoon and reaching up one hand to hoist himself into the Beaver's cabin.

Tears streaming down her face, she broke into a run. Beneath her sandaled feet the dock was slippery smooth. *Be careful,* her brain warned. *A fall could be dangerous.*

Hurry, her heart urged. *Don't let him leave.*

But she was already too late. The gap between plane and dock was widening, the span of wings turning in a slow circle as the pilot guided his craft into the bay. Swiping at the tears, she watched helplessly as the water foamed in the wake of the departing float plane. When it was no more than a speck in the sky, she slumped against the foot of the railing and buried her face in her hands.

To have come so close to paradise only to lose it was more than she could bear. The memories were just too painful, bringing alive again the feel of his hand at the nape of her neck, echoing his husky, low-pitched voice murmuring "Leila?" in perfect imitation of the real thing.

The sobs welled up, threatening to rip her apart. She wanted to sink into nothingness, bury herself in endless night.

But something — someone — called her back — "Leila...sweetheart." The hands that raised her to her feet were real, the shoulder against which she buried her face broad and welcoming, and the heart thumping unevenly beneath the solid wall of muscle, as tortured as her own.

"Leila, sweetheart," he said again.

Dazed, she dared to look up. "How are you here, Dante?" she whispered, her voice still drowning in tears. "You flew away."

Oh, the idiocy of the words! And how little they mattered when, after all, the only ones worth saying were, *I love you. Please don't ever leave me again.*

But he spoke first. "I couldn't leave you," he said, his mouth whispering over hers. "I promised myself I wouldn't pressure you to let me stay, but at the last minute, I just couldn't go.''

"But I saw you," she said on a hiccupping sob. "You climbed in the plane and left me."

He loomed over her in the dusk, his strength tempered by a humility she'd never seen in him before. "I'm nothing without you, my Leila, so I came back."

"Thank God you did," she said softly, touching her fingertips to his jaw, "because I think I might have died if you had not."

As if she weighed no more than a child, he scooped her up in his arms and strode back along the dock toward the house. Before she'd left for the Drummonds', she'd lighted citronella candles on the deck to ward off the mosquitoes. By their glow he navigated the steps and, settling himself on the sun chaise, held her firmly on his lap.

For the longest time he stayed with her there, holding her, kissing her hair, saying little things like, "I love you, I missed you, I'm a fool and I don't deserve you."

Twilight slipped unnoticed into the night. The party next door moved inside and let the frogs and crickets serenade the dark. At length the air grew cool and a chill crept over her that not even Dante's arms could dispel.

"I think we'd be more comfortable inside," she said.

"I'm afraid to move in case I wake up to find I've been dreaming and you're nothing but a fantasy."

"I'm real," she said, taking his hand and holding it a little to the left of her navel. "*We're* real. These are your babies romping around in here, Dante."

"Well, I'll be damned!" By the light of the citronella candles he gazed at her, his eyes full of awe. "I can actually feel the little devils playing football."

She stroked his cheek. "It's been a long time since their father kissed their mother."

He inched his mouth toward her in agonizing slow motion. "Like this, you mean?" he murmured, mes-

merizing her with the smoky intent in his voice, and
touched his lips to hers, blocking out the halo of candlelight surrounding his head and stealing her breath
away, even though the kiss was over before she'd begun
to tire of it.

"Not quite," she managed, as the spark she'd feared
could never be rekindled roared alive again.

His hand came up to capture her chin. "Then how
about this?"

Every part of her grew still. Her heart, her breathing,
the pulsing ache of desire he so easily aroused in her,
all hung in the balance as he brought his mouth to hers
a second time. And then, at the moment of actual contact, something inside her exploded, sending the blood
sizzling through her veins and the telltale moisture flooding between her thighs.

She clutched at the front of his shirt, helpless to stem
the moans rising low in her throat. Her lips opened to
the demands he made on them, her tongue welcomed his
with eager, pulsing little thrusts, and she was lost.

If he had flung her down on the bare wooden boards
of the deck and taken her, violently and without a shred
of feeling, she would have welcomed him. Because anything was better than the gnawing, empty yearning of
the last two months.

But he didn't. He seduced her with tenderness, kissing
her, stroking her, and whispering over and over that he'd
love her until he died and on through eternity.

Finally, when she was molten with desire and begging
with incoherent little cries for him to make love to her,
he swung to his feet and carried her through to the bedroom. "I want to make this last all night," he said, stripping away her clothes a layer at a time and branding
with his mouth each inch of bare skin as he exposed it,
"and savor every second."

But the fever that had her running her hands over
every lovely contour of his body was contagious.

Cursing with impatience, he flung off his own clothing and, catching her to him, buried himself inside her with one swift, sleek thrust.

"Tell me that I'll never lose you again," he begged, rocking against her.

"Never," she gasped, struggling to withstand the tide racing toward her and failing. The weight of him, the vigor, the driving, powerful strength, swept her into the undertow, filling all the lonely, empty corners of her heart and reviving her soul even as her body convulsed in helpless spasms beneath his.

It was the most purely lovely experience of her life.

"You know," he said afterward, lacing her fingers with his and pressing a kiss to her hand, "I'll be thirty-eight years old in September and I've spent most of them trying to compensate for the fact that I was born poor. You'd think I'd have learned differently a long time ago, but only since I met you have I realized that being rich has nothing to do with money. For that reason alone, I honor you, Leila, my love."

She turned on her side and snuggled close to him. "Do you?" she said, feeling him stir against her again. "Enough to make an honest woman out of me?"

"Oh, yes," he said raggedly, drawing her on top of him. "Just name the day and I'll be there."

Locked together in a harmony of perfect trust and passion, they at last got it right, making love with long, slow pleasure in each other, on a dot of an island in blue Canadian waters. And rediscovering with sleepy sensuality all those things which first had drawn them together on a speck of an island in the Caribbean.

The difference lay not in the miles separating one paradise from another, but in the certainty that comes of a woman belonging to the only man on earth who makes her feel whole.

She and Dante had more than a wedding day to look forward to. They had the rest of their lives. They had forever.

EXPECTING

She's sexy, she's successful... and she's pregnant!

Relax and enjoy these new stories about spirited women and gorgeous men, whose passion results in pregnancies... sometimes unexpectedly! All the new parents-to-be will discover that the business of making babies brings with it the most special love of all....

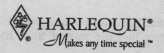

Look for a new and exciting series from Harlequin!

HARLEQUIN
Duets™

Two __new__ full-length novels in one book, from some of your favorite authors!

Starting in May, each month we'll be bringing you two new books, each book containing two brand-new stories about the lighter side of love! Double the pleasure, double the romance, for less than the cost of two regular romance titles!

Look for these two new Harlequin Duets™ titles in May 1999:

Book 1:
WITH A STETSON AND A SMILE
by Vicki Lewis Thompson
THE BRIDESMAID'S BET
by Christie Ridgway

Book 2:
KIDNAPPED? by Jacqueline Diamond
I GOT YOU, BABE by Bonnie Tucker

2 GREAT STORIES BY 2 GREAT AUTHORS FOR 1 LOW PRICE!

Don't miss it! Available May 1999 at your favorite retail outlet.

HARLEQUIN®
Makes any time special.™

Look us up on-line at: http://www.romance.net

HDGENR

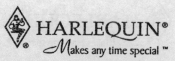

Coming Next Month

HARLEQUIN PRESENTS®

THE BEST HAS JUST GOTTEN BETTER!

#2019 PACIFIC HEAT Anne Mather
Olivia was staying with famous film star Diane Haran to write her biography, despite the fact that Diane had stolen Olivia's husband. Now Olivia planned to steal Diane's lover, Joe Castellano, by seduction...for revenge!

#2020 THE MARRIAGE DECIDER Emma Darcy
Amy had finally succumbed to a night of combustible passion with her impossibly handsome boss, Jake Carter. Now things were back to business as usual; he was still a determined bachelor...and she was pregnant....

#2021 A VERY PRIVATE REVENGE Helen Brooks
Tamar wanted her revenge on Jed Cannon, the notorious playboy who'd hurt her cousin. She'd planned to seduce him, then callously jilt him—but her plan went terribly wrong: soon it was marriage she wanted, not vengeance!

#2022 THE UNEXPECTED FATHER Kathryn Ross
(Expecting!)
Mom-to-be Samantha Walker was looking forward to facing her new life alone—but then she met the ruggedly handsome Josh Hamilton. But would they ever be able to overcome their difficult pasts and become a real family?

#2023 ONE HUSBAND REQUIRED! Sharon Kendrick
(Wanted: One Wedding Dress)
Ross Sheridan didn't know that his secretary, Ursula O'Neill, was in love with him until his nine-year-old daughter, Katie, played matchmaker.... Then it was only a matter of time before Katie was Ross and Ursula's bridesmaid!

#2024 WEDDING FEVER Lee Wilkinson
Raine had fallen in love with Nick Marlowe, not knowing the brooding American was anything but available. Years later, she was just about to marry another man when Nick walked back into Raine's life. And this time, he *was* single!